McCoy walked into the station house alone

He'd follow up with Heather Marshall personally tomorrow. Right now, however, she had him stymied. The superwoman wasn't pressing charges. Of course, *he'd* be pressing charges on behalf of the citizens of Houston. And she'd known that. Those perps wouldn't get away with violence.

She'd wanted to keep a low profile. No newspaper articles, nothing that would connect her to the safe haven or expose its location–her clients at the shelter needed to feel secure. He understood her point, but she could have been killed.

The thought made him sick. God knew she wasn't easy to deal with. Some might say pigheaded, and Officer Dave McCoy would be one of them. But she was alive. Passionate about everything. If he lived her way, he'd be exhausted. And out of a job.

Dear Reader,

When I was in my teens and twenties, I wanted to save the world. I still do.

This is exactly Heather Marshall's goal in my new story, *A Man of Honor,* when she rides in her van at night seeking out and helping runaway teenagers. In her jeans and sneakers, she looks like a kid herself. But she isn't the naive girl she used to be. Heather grew up with two alcoholic parents and, with a degree in social work and a black belt in kickboxing, she knows what she's doing on the streets.

Dave McCoy doesn't think so. He's the cop on the beat who's saved her hide more than once. Why can't she understand that a big city like Houston isn't as safe as that small west Texas town she's from?

I hope you enjoy watching these two strong people find their way to love and happiness.

Thanks so much for choosing to read *A Man of Honor.* I'm delighted that the editors at Harlequin Superromance believed in this story and in me. Happy reading!

Linda Barrett

P.S. I'd love to hear from you! Please e-mail me at linda@linda-barrett.com or write P.O. Box 1934, Houston, TX 77284-1934. Visit me on the Web at www.linda-barrett.com.

A Man of Honor

Linda Barrett

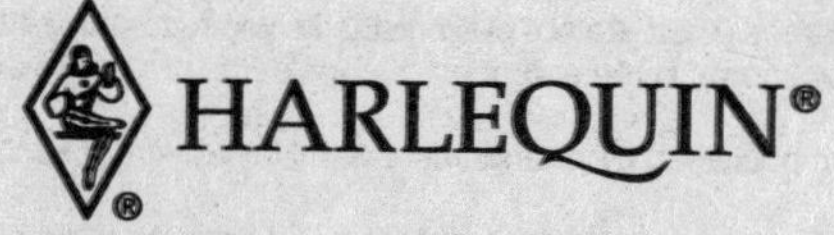

TORONTO • NEW YORK • LONDON
AMSTERDAM • PARIS • SYDNEY • HAMBURG
STOCKHOLM • ATHENS • TOKYO • MILAN • MADRID
PRAGUE • WARSAW • BUDAPEST • AUCKLAND

ISBN-13: 978-0-373-71366-0
ISBN-10: 0-373-71366-5

A MAN OF HONOR

This edition published by arrangement with Harlequin Books S.A.

www.eHarlequin.com

Printed in U.S.A.

ABOUT THE AUTHOR

Linda has been writing for pleasure all her adult life, but aimed for a professional career when she moved to Houston ten years ago. There she joined a local chapter of Romance Writers of America and attended so many workshops and seminars, she says, "I could have had a master's degree by now." Five years later, in 2001, Harlequin Superromance published her debut novel, *Love, Money and Amanda Shaw.* When not writing, the wife and mother of three grown sons ("all hero material like their dad") helps develop programs for a social service agency that works with the homeless.

Books by Linda Barrett

HARLEQUIN SUPERROMANCE

971–LOVE, MONEY AND AMANDA SHAW
1001–TRUE-BLUE TEXAN
1073–THE APPLE ORCHARD
1115–THE INN AT OAK CREEK*
1192–THE HOUSE ON THE BEACH*
1218–NO ORDINARY SUMMER*
1256–RELUCTANT HOUSEMATES*
1289–THE DAUGHTER HE NEVER KNEW*

*Pilgrim Cove

To my son David,
who knows how to laugh,
who sees the best in everyone
and who survived being the middle child.
I love you.

PROLOGUE

Dry Creek, West Texas

HEATHER MARSHALL slammed the door of the house she called the pit and ran down the country road, wanting to follow it forever. Tears flowed down her face. With a hard stroke, she wiped them away, then pressed her right side where her father's fist had connected. She knew the impact would cause a colorful bruise that would last for days.

She paused a half mile away at the cutoff leading to town and limped toward the familiar limestone rock where she'd wait for her sister. The limestone formed a natural bench, and Heather sat down heavily. She wrapped her arms around herself. January evenings were cold in West Texas, and she'd had no time to grab her jacket.

Oh, God! What could she do? Her parents. A couple of alcoholics. And if alcoholism was a disease, as folks said, George and Jolene sure didn't care about curing it. Neither did the others who partied with them.

As she waited, the occasional car passed by. Drivers waved and Heather waved back as if nothing was wrong. Pretending. Just as they did. Everyone in town knew the Marshalls, but neighbors mostly minded their own business. Mostly. Except not a month ago when her dad lost his job. Then, everyone knew everything because George Marshall had been a deputy sheriff for the town of Dry Creek.

Heather spotted the big headlights of the local bus, stood up and ran toward it. A minute later, Kathy got off.

"What happened this time?" she asked, wrapping her sweater around Heather's shoulders.

"He's drunk," replied Heather, her voice trembling. "Very, very drunk. He broke a lamp, and he's…swinging…hitting everything and… He's a monster and there's nowhere to hide."

"Shh." Kathy put her arm around her sister. "He's worse since he was dumped from the force."

"At least they took his gun away."

"If only Mama had the guts to throw him out," said Kathy. "She's what's called an 'enabler.' I've been studying, doing some research."

Heather nodded, but the news didn't make her feel any better. Kathy liked studying so much—was so good at it—she'd won a college scholarship for next year. In Houston.

"Kath," she whispered, "what am I going to do when you're gone?"

"Oh, sweetie," Kathy replied, holding her close. "Leaving you behind is killing me. But…I've got to get out of this place."

Heather leaned against her big sister. "Then take me with you. Twelve is old enough."

Kathy didn't reply at first. Then a tear landed on Heather's cheek. A second one followed. And then another. Finally, Kathy choked out a response. "I can't, Heather. I just can't."

CHAPTER ONE

Fifteen years later

HEATHER DROVE SLOWLY along the service road of the busy Katy Freeway. Her unmarked van was filled with supplies—food, water, toiletries, blankets—she'd packed before starting her rounds that evening. A full mobile pantry testified to the money-stretching skill she'd honed since childhood. And now she was using it to help other kids. Kids in trouble. Runaways.

Her gaze shifted from the traffic ahead of her to the parking lots alongside the Houston interstate. She'd developed keen night vision to spot her delicate quarry.

A group of youngsters stood waiting for her to pull into the driveway of a tired-looking strip mall, one of her usual stops. She recognized two girls—Brenda and Alicia—and wanted to cheer. Return visits meant trust…at least some trust. Without it, she'd fail, despite her best intentions.

She turned into the mall and pulled forward, parking parallel to the road, careful not to block the driveway. She shut off the motor and groaned when it groaned. That would take more money to fix, but she'd worry about it later. She grabbed a box of PBJ sandwiches and chips, pushed the door open and stepped out.

"Hey, y'all. I'm so-o-o glad to see ya. Who's hungry?" She reached into her carton, distributed the items, studying the youngsters as casually as possible.

Youngsters? A few of the new boys seemed older. Or maybe it was the expression on their faces that made her think so. She turned to Brenda. "Going to introduce me to your friends? Or...aren't y'all together?"

Alicia spoke up. "Oh, yeah, we are. These guys got a place to live. So we don't have to eat up your sandwiches anymore. We just wanted to say bye to you and thanks."

"Baby G, you talk too much," snapped one of the new members of the group.

"Sorry," Alicia whispered, looking at the ground.

The dynamics had changed in the past few days and not for the better. "What's going on?" she asked Brenda, the more confident of the two girls.

Brenda shrugged. "We got a place of our own

now. And jobs. Easy jobs. That's all." She looked away. "Ask them."

Heather turned to the three newcomers.

"Like the girls said, they're with us now, and we'll take care of them." One male stepped forward. The leader, in posture and gesture. Letting her know what's what. Possibly he thought she'd go looking for the kids if they didn't show up. Maybe get the cops involved. "We're just letting them say goodbye to the nice lady. Because we're nice boys. Right?"

His two cohorts chuckled, but Heather focused on the speaker. In his twenties, Latin, husky build, a couple of inches taller than her. "And you are…?"

He grinned, full of confidence and machismo, before his expression turned hungry, like a rattlesnake tasting the air. His dark eyes traveled slowly down her body and back up. His easy grin became a sickle-shaped smile, sharp and predatory. He stared at her without blinking.

She met his gaze head-on, but goose bumps burst out all over her skin. She could probably handle one of them. But three? She rocked on the balls of her feet, ready to run.

The man cocked his head before replying. "Just

call me *el Jefe*—the boss." He nodded at the girls Heather had been helping. "Go. Jet outta here."

The kids obeyed instantly.

Heather heard cars passing along the service road, and one actually entered the lot. But the driver kept going, intent on finding a parking space closer to the set-back stores. Probably never noticed her. And neither would anyone else.

Heather stepped backward—closer to her van. "I've got more stops to make," she said. "People will be looking for me. If you're hungry, grab a sandwich. Take the whole box." She tossed it to the leader, who let the food hit the ground. She inched backward again, glad she'd left the door open.

"No, *chica*. No van," he said, swaggering toward her until he was only a few feet away. He pointed at one of his friends, and nodded toward the vehicle. "Take a look."

Look for what? Blankets? Heather watched in disbelief, her anger rising, as the man got in her van. She'd worked hard on this mobile outreach project. "What do you think I've got in there?" she demanded. "Drugs?"

The "boss" and his cohort outside the van loomed closer, and she groaned silently. When would she learn to keep her mouth shut? And why hadn't she been able to find a partner tonight? She heard the third man rummaging in her vehicle. Heard him behind her when he called out.

"*Mira,* amigos. Look what she keeps for playtime. All different colors, too."

The box of condoms. For the kids who asked her. So children wouldn't have children.

El jefe's eyes lit up. "A consolation prize," he said, "from the beautiful lady."

Bile rose to her throat, but she forced it down.

He reached toward his waist, snapped his wrist, and metal gleamed in the light of the streetlamp. He held a knife with a long ugly blade.

"Into the van, Ms. Heather. And no noise."

They could drive away with her. They might kill her. But to go quietly?

"No-o-o!" she screamed at the top of her lungs, running at the man, counting on surprise to give her an advantage. She kicked him flat-footed in his solar plexus, and he stumbled, giving her space to spin around and kick him a second time. Directly in the groin. He doubled over, howling, and dropped the knife.

She targeted the other two men, each with similar

weapons in their hands. By the feral light in their eyes, she could tell they wanted her blood.

She was screwed.

OFFICER DAVE MCCOY approached quietly. The players were so intent on their drama, they hadn't noticed him yet. He hadn't been flying lights or sirens, merely cruising the freeway as part of his patrol. But he'd recognized Heather Marshall's van, held together with spit, as he'd mentioned to her on numerous occasions.

When he spotted it, he'd slowed to make sure she hadn't broken down. He hadn't planned on stopping. He knew she wanted him to stay away from "her" kids. Except when he cut his wheel to enter the lot, he'd heard her scream. He'd braked hard and quickly made his way around the back of her van in time to see her connect with some guy's family jewels and a weapon fall to the ground. The other two thugs pulled their knives and he ran forward, gun in hand. "Drop them." He hoped his voice was as menacing as his weapon.

As one, they turned toward him. Then Heather raced to kick the knife away from the guy on the ground.

Dave kept his eyes on the men, but spoke to the woman. "Get behind me…go to my car and call for backup. Code 8. When you tell them I can't get to the radio, they'll be here in seconds."

He sensed her disappearing behind the van. "I said drop those knives. Now!" he barked.

One hit the floor.

He waited a heartbeat and aimed his weapon at the suspect still holding his knife. "Resisting arrest. I'll start with your knee…."

The knife dropped. "Smart boy. Both of you—put your hands on your heads." Now his voice was quiet, full of authority. "You're going to stand there nice and easy…because I just had target practice today…and I'm damn near perfect…." And just as he'd predicted, it didn't take two minutes until he heard the sweet blare of sirens closing in.

The perps heard it, too. "Smart boy" turned and sprinted toward the row of stores at the back of the lot. And out of the corner of his eye, Dave saw a blond whirlwind fly after the guy. "No!" she screamed at him.

"Let him go!" Dave yelled. The woman was putting herself in more danger, and he could do nothing at the moment.

But then his buddies arrived—Powers, Jazzman, Yorkie and two others. "Cuff these two," Dave ordered as he sprinted after Heather. "Bring 'em in. Weapons are on the ground, but search them again. And Miranda them. One of you follow me."

Heather was gaining on the guy. The few shoppers on foot quickly got out of the way. Between Heather giving chase, and the people watching him, the suspect seemed to get confused. Dave veered left to cut him off, his timing perfect. The perp almost ran into his arms. Dave turned him and cuffed his hands behind his back.

And there stood Heather Marshall. Unstoppable. Her blond hair in disarray, sexy enough to raise any man's blood pressure. She came straight at the cuffed man, her hands fisted.

"Where are my kids?" she screamed.

"She's crazy, man. Loco," mumbled the perp.

"Answer her."

"We didn't do nothin' to those kids." The man indicated with his head. "See? *Mira*." He stared over Heather's shoulder.

"Are those yours?" asked Dave.

Heather turned. Her smile answered him.

"Jazzman," called Dave, "take this suspect into custody." He watched his buddy haul the guy off, heard him begin, "You have the right to remain silent...." That was enough for Dave.

He turned back to Heather, who hadn't moved, simply staring at the teens. "Ms. Marshall?"

She looked up at him, her face pale in the dim light, her lips trembling. So unlike her usual self. "McCoy," she said in a small voice, "I—I don't feel well...." He caught her before she hit the ground.

HEATHER HEARD high-pitched voices and a single low one. She opened her eyes to see McCoy kneeling next to her, his intense gaze tinged with concern. She felt his fingers on her wrist.

"Come on, Heather, breathe. Inhale. Exhale. That's it. No more sleeping."

The ground felt hard under her body. She slowly turned her head and realized she was still in the parking lot. Alicia and Brenda stood nearby. She began to push herself to a sitting position, and felt a strong arm around her, assisting her.

"This is ridiculous," she murmured, now upright. "I've never fainted in my life."

"You've probably never taken on three hoods in your life, either," replied McCoy, "and all at the same time. I guarantee your adrenaline shot through the clouds and then crashed. An occupational hazard for cops." He paused, fingers still on her wrist. "Your pulse is normal now, but we've called an ambulance. The medics should be right here."

"No way," she protested weakly. She got to her feet, then wished she hadn't. Nausea made her sway.

"Would you take it easy for a change?" McCoy's impatience sounded too familiar to Heather, but his firm hand steadied her.

Why did it have to be McCoy who showed up? She didn't like the man—which was fair because he sure didn't like her, either. She had to tolerate him, though, because he was the cop on the beat where she and Kathy had lived and worked for the past four years. He'd proven helpful when they'd needed him at Welcome Home, the women's shelter they ran. But his quiet ability to make people do what he wanted them to—so different from her father's loud abuse—scared her. McCoy was a controlling cop. In the end, he and George were the same.

"What were you thinking, Heather? How could you go out without a partner? Again. How many times have I...?" He shook his head, frustration clearly written on his face.

His voice wasn't quiet tonight.

She stood on her own now. "What happened to Ms. Marshall?" she asked, seeking to divert him.

"Try acting like an intelligent adult," he began, cut off by the ambulance's screaming approach.

"I'm not going to the hospital," said Heather. "Absolutely not. I'm feeling much stronger. Healthy as a horse."

"And more stubborn than a mule." His sigh was huge. "Why don't you let the medics make the call? In fact, you might prefer the hospital."

"Prefer?"

He nodded. "We're going to have a little talk, Ms. Heather Marshall. Just as soon as you're up to it." He added something under his breath.

"What was that?" she asked.

He didn't reply.

"Do you insult every law-abiding person on your beat?" she asked, her anger mounting. "I am *not* a child."

His eyebrows rose to meet his hairline. "I'll let that pass. But you're going to listen because what I've got to offer is a lot of common sense. Something you sorely need."

The medics arrived then, preventing Heather from retorting. Five minutes later they pronounced her vital signs strong and, when she refused to accompany them to the E.R., they left.

Brenda and Alicia walked slowly toward her, their heads cocked to watch Dave at the same time. "Ms. Heather," said Alicia, "I think I want to call my mama. I want to go home, and I don't care what Brenda thinks."

"I didn't say nothin'," said Brenda. "I'm going to the Youth Center across town. It's better than goin' home. I ain't never goin' back home." She raised her chin as if to dare anyone to say otherwise.

"That's fine," said Heather quickly. "Sometimes home isn't the best place."

The familiar comfort of helping the youngsters enwrapped her like a soft flannel blanket. Helping them was what she did best. Dealing with Officer McCoy was another matter.

HEATHER GLANCED in her rearview mirror. Yup. The cop was following her to the women's shelter. Five minutes later, she paused in the driveway of Welcome Home, pressed the button and waited for the chain-link fence to slide open. "Thanks, Diana," she said into the speaker. "I'm not coming in tonight. Going straight home from here."

Before leaving the van, however, she took the time to fill out a trip form, which included miles traveled, number of teens helped, amount of supplies used. The raw data would help to establish the need for teen services. McCoy was waiting for her when she drove her Neon from the lot. Furious, she pulled over to the curb and got out.

"Don't you have anything better to do?" she snapped. "I can make my own way home."

"Simply doing my job," he replied in a calm voice.

"Look, McCoy," she began. "You were really great back there, and I appreciate your help. But—"

"How about you getting back behind the wheel," he interrupted, "so I can follow you home and call it a night?"

Without saying a word, she got back in her car and slammed the door shut. What choice did she have? She had to get home before Kathy called the police. It was after eleven. The cop hadn't lied. McCoy worked 4:00 p.m. to midnight, and his shift really was coming to an end. He'd spent a lot of it on her.

The entrance light glowed over the door as she pulled in front of the small house she shared with her sister. Kathy's car sat in the driveway, with Mark's Lexus behind it. When Heather was home, Kathy's fiancé normally parked in the street, leaving the driveway for the women. He must have stayed later than he'd planned that evening.

Her mind raced. Now, she'd have to explain her adventure to both of them if they saw McCoy. Well, McCoy wasn't going inside, so maybe they wouldn't have to know about her evening at all. The less Kathy knew, the better. Between her upcoming December wedding and Welcome Home, Kathy shouldn't have to worry about Heather, too.

Heather left her vehicle and walked toward McCoy, who was standing next to his patrol car. She pasted a smile on her face. "You can go home now, McCoy. Thanks."

He inclined his head toward a spot behind her. "Not so fast," he replied with a smile.

Kathy and Mark were striding down the front walk toward them.

"Damn it!" said Heather, her temper rising at McCoy's sense of humor. She glared at him. "I'll do the talking, McCoy."

But Mark cut her off before she could start. "Your sister's worn a hole in the rug from pacing. Is there any law that can keep her off the streets this late?"

"Late? It's only just past eleven o'clock," said Heather.

The cop shook his head. "I suggest you form the Heather Marshall Safety Committee. At least insist on her having a partner. The woman doesn't understand that a city as big as Houston is not safe like the small town she's used to."

"What happened tonight?" asked Kathy, looking from Heather to McCoy. "Was it the van again?"

"Ms. Marshall will explain everything," Dave said. "I'm going to file my reports."

And just like that, he was gone.

Kathy turned to Heather. "What kind of reports does he have to file?"

"It was nothing. Come on inside and I'll tell you." An expunged version.

By the time they reached the kitchen, she'd decided how to restructure the story. She left out the knives, the fainting spell. McCoy happened to be passing by—a truthful statement—and overreacted to the boys, not men. "You know I can take care of myself," she said, glancing from Kathy to Mark. She stretched and flexed her arms. "I've trained in kickboxing."

Mark stood in the doorway, shoulder against the wall, his posture as casual as his attitude seemed to be.

"And exactly why," he began slowly, "are we speaking about fighting skills right now?"

"Oh, my God!" said Kathy, grasping Heather's arm. "Something really did happen tonight." Her eyes filled immediately, and Heather hugged her tight.

"I'm fine, Kath. I promise. It was nothing."

"Officer McCoy suggested you take a partner, Heather," said Mark. "And that makes sense to me."

She looked up at the man. "I had a partner, but she backed out. I couldn't *not* show up for the kids. End of story."

"Do you want me to hire a security guard to go with her?" Mark asked Kathy.

"No!" Heather took a deep breath. "Of course not." Mark came from Texas royalty—ran a successful pipeline company for the oil industry. But she had no call on his funds.

"Let's calm down," said Heather, modulating her voice while her thoughts raced at Mach speed. "I've been going out in the van for the past two years. So, what's really changed?"

Kathy jumped up from her chair as though burned. Her dark eyes blazed, her hands fisted at her sides. "You want to know what's changed? I'll tell you—the van's falling apart now, and you could be stranded anywhere—backstreets, dark parks—wherever the heck you go. You're staying out later than you used to, and you used to arrange for a lot of volunteers to help. You've either forgotten about that, or you're too busy, but I don't like the results. And that's just for starters.

"At work, you flag in the afternoons, and I need you at full strength. Welcome Home is our first priority. We have contracts to fulfill for those women and their children. They are our clients." Kathy's breath was labored, and Heather held up her hand. "No, I won't stop," continued Kathy. "Because more important, I love you, Heather. You're the only sister I have, and I can't lose you."

Tears trickled down Kathy's face. Heather reached for her sister and wiped her tears away. Then she felt Kathy's fingers on her own cheeks.

"You're crying, too," whispered Kathy, squeezing her tight. "This girl never cries."

"Good thing I don't have sisters," said Mark. "W-a-y too emotional for a guy like me."

Heather gave him a thumbs-up and a wobbly grin. "All we need is a new van," she said. "And you'll be happy again, right?"

"It's a start," said Kathy. "Know someone in the car business?"

Heather tapped her mouth with her forefinger. "No, but how about private funding?"

"Heather, every dollar we raise right now is for Welcome Home. I'm not screwing around with funding sources. We could lose donors or be shut down for transferring funds."

"No, no. Of course not from the shelter," Heather replied quickly. "But how about Sara Patterson? She's got a birthday coming up. Perfect timing."

Heather looked at her sister and grinned. An identical grin crossed Kathy's face. "See why I love working with her?" Kathy said to Mark. "She's the creative problem solver. I'm the dry administrator. We're a great team."

"Sweetheart," said Mark, with a gleam in his eye, "I think you're pretty darn creative."

The two sisters looked at each other and rolled their eyes.

"I don't get it," Mark added. "If it's Sara's birthday, why would you get a van? Doesn't she get the presents?"

"Nope," said Heather. "She throws herself a party and tells all the guests to make checks payable to her favorite charity."

"Let's make sure it's us this year," Kathy said.

"A very unique approach," admitted Mark. "How'd you meet such a woman?"

"Heck, we knew her in Dry Creek. Same age as Heather," replied Kathy. "She was as miserable in that dusty town as we were and practically took the next bus out of there after Heather's, right after they graduated high school. She stayed with us in Houston for a little while, before her career took off."

"She's a real estate mogul," added Heather. "I tease her about it all the time. The poor country girl makes good in the big city." She reached for the phone.

"It's late on a work night," Mark said. "You could frighten her by calling now."

"Sara's evening is just getting started. She parties a lot." Sure enough, Sara answered on the first ring. And five minutes later, they had a sponsor for the van.

She left her sister and Mark in the kitchen and made her way down the hall to her bedroom, flopping on the bed, exhausted. She wouldn't give up on the kids. Not ever.

She closed her eyes and unexpectedly images of the big cop filled her head. Dave McCoy. What the hell did he know about living in a small town? Safe, huh? He didn't know sic 'em from c'mere about a small town. And he didn't know anything about her, either. Which was just the way she wanted it.

DAVE WALKED into the station house alone, his mind on the report he'd file. He'd follow up with Heather Marshall personally the next day or night. Right now, however, she had him stymied. The super-woman wasn't pressing charges. Of course, *he'd* be pressing charges on behalf of the citizens of Houston. And she'd known that. The perps wouldn't get away with violence.

She'd wanted to keep a low profile for the sake of Welcome Home. No newspaper articles or items on the police action sheets. Nothing that would connect her to the safe haven and expose its location. Her clients at the shelter needed to feel secure. He understood her point, but was surprised just the same. She could've been killed.

The thought made him sick. God knew she wasn't easy to deal with. Some might say pigheaded, and he'd be one of them. But she was alive. Passionate about everything: her work, family, the kids. If he lived her way, he'd be exhausted. And out of a job. Dave's reputation as a dependable cop rested on his ability to remain calm and in control.

By the time Dave reached his desk, he knew the thugs were behind bars clamoring for their lawyers. He'd also been slapped on the back by almost everyone in the station house.

As Dave picked up a pen to begin writing, Powers and Jazzman, his backup, came over ready to discuss the incident. And Heather Marshall.

"I never saw anything like it," Powers said.

"Where is she now?" asked Jazzman.

"Home. She insisted on driving that godforsaken van back to the shelter. I stayed on her tail until she walked through her own front door."

"Hell," Jazzman said, nudging Powers, "I would have stayed on her tail, too."

The guys laughed. "That is one fine-looking woman," Powers agreed.

"Enough," Dave growled.

"An Amazon," Jazzman said, louder.

"She's only this tall," protested Dave, touching his chest. "Exactly."

His buddies grinned at each other. "Exactly?" asked Powers. "And how do we know that?"

Damn. Dave felt his ears start to burn. "Knock it off."

His friends didn't budge. "Okay," said Dave, "she passed out and I couldn't let her fall.... Oh, what the hell. You both know the neighborhood. You must know the Marshall sisters."

"Yeah, but…uh…we're not that up close and personal. It's your beat. We're just neighbors. But if you want to trade off with me…?" Powers raised his voice suggestively.

"Get out of here and let me do my work."

Laughing, his buddies finally left him in peace. But Dave couldn't concentrate. He kept picturing Heather, alone, surrounded by those men. With knives. A lucky kick to the groin bought her time, but there was no defense against a well-aimed blade or bullet.

CHAPTER TWO

WHEN HEATHER OPENED her eyes the next morning, the sun shone brightly into her room. The house seemed quiet. Too quiet. She checked the clock radio on her night table, jumped out of bed and ran to the kitchen. Kathy had left a note on the fridge saying to take her time, and she'd see her at work.

But Heather had a group to lead at ten o'clock, a mere thirty-five minutes from now. She washed quickly, pulled on a pair of jeans and plain knit jersey, jumped into the car and arrived at the shelter with eight minutes to spare.

Welcome Home sat on one acre surrounded by a ten-foot fence. The two-story brick building used to be an old school. Kathy and Heather had made the building and land part of their proposal for federal funding in the grant they'd written five years ago. Since opening the shelter, Heather pinched herself each time she went to work in the morning. Heck, she pinched herself every time she thought about her life. Childhood had definitely been overrated.

She parked in her assigned spot, locked her car and walked around to the front door. A camera perched above the entrance; others were strategically placed around the building, outside and in. Visitors were admitted by security personnel who guarded the premises 24/7, sitting by a bank of monitors at the front desk.

"Hey, Trish," she greeted the day shift guard. "Anything happen that I should know about?"

"Mornin' Heather. When I came on at seven, Diana told me she'd had a quiet night."

Heather grinned, thinking of *her* night. "Just the way we like them."

"Yes, ma'am."

"I've got a group in five minutes, but page me if you need to." Heather pushed open the steel door to the administrative wing, heard it clang shut as she walked down the corridor to her office. Kathy's office was diagonally across from hers, and beyond theirs was payroll-accounting, fund-raising and the switchboard.

She put her purse in a file drawer and glanced at the folders on her desk. Each one represented a new resident. The women she worked with needed so much…she had so much responsibility here at Welcome Home. And yet, she couldn't give up her work with the runaway kids. No matter what anyone else said.

She patted a very fat folder labeled: GIRL-FRIENDS—A SHELTER FOR TEENAGE GIRLS. Inside it were copies of the funding applications she'd submitted to the federal and state governments. The awards would be announced Friday, posted on the Internet, and her nerves got the best of her whenever she thought about it. Was she crazy to start something new? To start over again with another shelter?

She thought about her childhood in Dry Creek. About her father, big George Marshall. About how she herself had tried to run away. Except she'd been caught. She inhaled deeply. Then again. Kids needed a safe place. She'd find a way to do everything.

The phone rang. It was an outside call.

"Heather Marshall speaking."

"I need a place to…I need…help. My kids aren't… Please. Can you help me?" The woman sounded frantic.

"Talk to me," said Heather in a calm tone. "Where are you?"

"A pay phone, downtown, near the bus transit

center. My husband went to work, and we're getting out. I can barely walk. I c-can't take it anymore."

"Get on the west side bus to the Katy Freeway," said Heather slowly. "Get off at Campbell Road. Look for a white van. My name is Heather, and I will meet you. Or I can send someone to pick you up where you are right now."

"I'll take the bus."

Heather made the woman repeat the directions. "How old are the kids?"

"Seven and ten."

"Okay. No problem."

"And one more thing…" The woman on the phone hesitated.

"Yes?" prompted Heather.

"My husband…he's the one…well, he's…he's a Houston cop. And no one will believe me. Can I still come there?" Her last words tumbled over one another.

"Of course," Heather replied instantly. "You and your children are very welcome here."

"Thank God. Thank you. I've been calling everywhere."

Strange. Heather replaced the receiver slowly and took the folders into Kathy's office. She told her about the new resident.

"I said I'd pick her up in the van, so can you take my group? Or should I get one of the counselors to cover?"

"I'll do it." Kathy's expression was thoughtful.

"What?" asked Heather.

Kathy stood up. "I hate to say this, but having a cop's wife here could get…complicated. Even dangerous to our anonymity if her husband's intent on tracking her down. He's an abuser who's also a cop. He'll know how to find us."

Heather hadn't thought of that. That was why the woman had been forced to make several calls. The Police Department was a good friend to Welcome Home and to all the shelters in the city. The cops knew the locations because they often transported abuse victims to these safe places. They were usually very supportive.

"But," continued Kathy, putting her arm around Heather, "you did the right thing. We can't let one man, even if he is a cop, prevent us from doing our job and helping his wife. And besides, Houston is a big city…."

"We've got security," added Heather. "If he does find us, he won't get in."

"Right," said Kathy, taking the file folders. "Now I'll go meet the group, while you get our new family."

THE BUS ARRIVED ten minutes after Heather did. She spotted Welcome Home's clients immediately by the bulging backpacks on the kids, the stuffed tote bag on the mother's arm. The sum total of their lives. She walked toward them quickly, knowing the woman would feel better the sooner she was out of sight.

"I'm Heather Marshall. Are you the person I spoke with earlier?"

Dark glasses hid the woman's eyes, but she nodded. "Mary Beth Landers," she whispered.

Heather led them the few feet to the van, chatting to the children. "In you go," she urged, sliding the door open. "Buckle yourselves into a seat while I help Mom." She turned toward Mary Beth. "Let's put the tote in the van first and then get you in."

Mary Beth nodded.

"Grab the bar and step up on your good leg… that's it." The woman slowly maneuvered herself into the passenger seat. Heather saw tears trickling down Mary Beth's cheeks, but whether they were from physical pain or emotional release, she couldn't tell. "We'll get you some medical attention today if possible," said Heather as she put the van in motion. "As soon as you settle in."

"Settle in?"

"That's right. You can stay for as long as you need to."

"But you don't understand. I…we…can't stay in Houston. He'll find us. They'll find us. The police. They all stick together. Every cop is his friend. Oh, my God. I can't believe what's happening to us." She turned and reached a hand toward her children, and her tears flowed in force. The little girl started to sob, then her brother joined in.

Oh, dear. This wasn't going to be easy. Despite Heather's initial confidence, she now realized that they may have gotten into a predicament they had no experience in handling. She passed around a box of tissues as she continued driving. North. West. And a few blocks north again until she pulled into the shelter's driveway.

"Okay, everyone. Take a look outside at where you'll be staying. See the fence, kids? No one gets in without permission. Just watch."

Heather went through the admission procedure with Security, glanced at her passengers' expressions when they saw how the gate had to mechanically slide open. "See. Only the guard inside can open it."

The boy shook his head. "My dad's big." He raised his arms to the roof of the van. "He can climb over."

"No one ever has," said Heather. "And no one—

not one single person—has ever gotten inside unless we wanted him to."

The boy had stopped crying by then, and Heather continued to chat to the children, knowing full well that their mom was listening to every word. She pointed out the surveillance cameras, the ten-foot fences. She turned right after the entrance and drove around to the back door where the kids could see the playground equipment and picnic tables.

"Ooh, Mommy. This is nice." Megan seemed to be distracted easily enough. At least for now.

"There are some other children living here, too," said Heather.

"My age?" asked the boy, whose name, Heather had learned, was Neil.

"I believe so. But not as tall as you, buddy."

The kid grinned, and Heather had to chuckle. Too bad size had nothing to do with a man's worth.

"We're going to get you settled into your own private apartment. We have forty units here," said Heather, leading the family inside.

There were a score of things to do for these people, and she needed to assign a case manager. The special circumstances might put a staff member at risk—not that any one of them would refuse to work with the new residents. Regardless, Heather would take on the new family herself.

An hour later, she let Kathy know. They were lunching in her sister's office.

"I figured you would," Kathy said, before biting into her sandwich.

"Amazing," replied Heather. "I didn't know it myself until after I met them."

Kathy smiled. "You always take the hardest ones. Do you think we should get McCoy involved on the q.t.? He might be able to keep tabs on the husband for us."

Heather dropped the orange she'd just peeled. "Not on your life. Mary Beth is terrified of the entire police department. I can't make an exception and I won't lie to her. Besides, we don't know how McCoy would react. He's part of that fraternity, too."

"I think you underestimate him, Heather. He's been a friend to Welcome Home from the beginning."

"Oh, please," said Heather, separating her orange into sections. "It's easy to be a 'friend' when your own friends aren't involved. He's had nothing at stake in the past. Welcome Home is merely in his territory, part of his job."

Kathy's forehead puckered as she balled up her

napkin and threw it in the trash. "Well, I was very glad he helped you last night, and I believe he'd do his job now, too. But you're in charge of the Landers case, and it's your call. If you change your mind, let me know immediately."

"I won't. I don't trust any cop, including McCoy." She grinned at her sister, then popped an orange section into her mouth, content with her morning.

Kathy stared at her. "Don't let Dry Creek ruin your judgment. Dad certainly wasn't a role model for law enforcement."

"Heck, Kathy. He wasn't a role model for humanity." She waved her hand in dismissal. "Would it surprise you to know alcoholism runs rampant in police departments? So does divorce. And then there's the control—"

"New topic," said Kathy, "before we're buried in our own work again."

Heather grudgingly nodded.

"The van's off limits," said Kathy. "Gene looked at it early this morning. It's a money pit." Thank God their facilities manager knew a lot about cars.

"I have classes tonight," Heather began, "but I'm scheduled to make my rounds tomorrow night. I guess I'll take my car. Problem solved until Sara raises lots of money for us."

"Your car?" Kathy shook her head. "You'd better take mine...."

Her sister was the best. Kathy's car was newer, bigger. "Thanks. Thanks a lot. I'll be able to haul more stuff with yours."

"And in return for the favor," said Kathy, her tone capturing Heather's full attention, "you'll go dress shopping with me this Saturday. You, my maid of honor, have still not bought a dress." Kathy's eyes sparkled with mischief as Heather groaned. A real waste of time for an off-the-rack kind of girl.

THE TYPE-A'S WERE already in the briefing room that afternoon by the time Dave arrived with fifteen minutes to spare before roll call. He made his way to the phone to check his voice mail before grabbing one of the old plastic chairs in the cluttered room. Sitting, he got ready to jot notes on his clipboard about anything pertinent to his upcoming watch.

Then he waited for the rest of the shift to show up. They'd have a thirty-minute meeting, get car assignments—and he'd be on his way.

"Hey, McCoy."

"Hey, Yorkie." Eve Hannity, born and raised in the Bronx until she was ten years old and moved to Texas, still carried her New York inflection. Everyone called her Yorkie. As she said, "It could've been worse. How about terrier?" She was a good cop and a good friend.

"What's up?" he asked.

She nodded at the podium. "He's announcing the sergeant's exam today. I'm gonna crack the books. You?"

He'd known the announcement was due, but hadn't thought about it lately. A promotion would take him off the streets a lot. And he liked the streets. But the pay was a lot better and… And what the hell was he thinking? Of course, he wanted a promotion. A career path. Just like his dad, who'd retired as a lieutenant from the same department.

"If you're setting up a couple of study sessions, Yorkie, I'm in."

She high-fived him. "One more thing." She faced the room at large. "Hey, everybody. Listen up. Larry and I are throwing a little barbecue this Saturday night. For those of you who aren't working, come on over. My sister's visiting—maybe relocating—and she's single, guys. And cute, if I do say so myself."

She turned back to Dave. “You’ll like her. And what’s more. She’ll like you.”

Drops of sweat broke out on his lip. “Stop right there. I’m not looking—”

“And neither is she. You can relax. Lisa just wants to have a good time with nice people. Have some fun. I’m not trading in my badge for a matchmaking license.”

He breathed a bit easier. But not much.

“You must be hard up for friends, if all you can come up with is a bunch of cops to invite.”

“Watch it, McCoy. You’re talking about my other family here,” replied Yorkie with a grin.

Sergeant Novak went to the podium and the chatter and shuffling in the room stopped almost instantly. Now Dave and the shift would hear about internal memos and learn the latest from the streets before they went out on patrol.

Yorkie had called it. The sergeant exam was announced and a quiet buzz filled the air. Yorkie’s party would be the scene for setting up a study group and schedule.

“Listen up, you guys and gals. Here goes.” The sergeant read the list of restraining orders, stolen vehicles, stolen guns while Dave and the others took notes. "And the final item we have relates to last night's incident on the Katy Freeway."

Every eye was on Novak. The silence pounded in Dave's ears.

"Six of you responded to the call, a female adult citizen. The situation also involved two female minors and three adult male perpetrators, who are now in jail. However, we have reason to believe four perps were involved. Not three."

McCoy's gut tightened. Could he have missed a suspect last night? Was he so distracted that he lost focus?

"The youths told Officer Powers four men lived in the apartment where they stayed over the weekend and that all four had gone to the strip mall," continued the sergeant. "The suspect who was injured by the citizen has made a lot of noise about his brother seeking revenge for the arrests. He's also cursing the woman."

"She sure got him where it hurts," someone murmured.

Novak paused and looked out over the group. "The suspect has a hot temper and could just be blowing hot air, but we believe there's a new drug operation in town, ladies and gents, and their goal is to move the junk. Part of a larger cartel. These guys are young, however, and they've already made mistakes. Let's weed them out before they take root."

Dave was all for that.

"And McCoy?"

"Sergeant?"

"Even though the three perps aren't going anywhere for a while, despite their lawyers clamoring for bail…I want the citizen advised about the threat. I'm assigning an additional patrol to your area until further notice." He looked at Eve. "Get with McCoy afterward and split the beat."

He looked at his notes. "And McCoy, you contact…Ms. Heather Marshall. Advise her to use extra caution until we find out more about the brother."

Dave nodded. With this new information, there was an outside chance she'd listen to him.

HEATHER'S OFFICE PHONE rang at four-thirty just as she was preparing to leave for class.

"I've got Officer McCoy out front here," said Trish. "He's asked to see you."

She wasn't in the mood for a lecture about her van, or about last night. She'd give him one minute. "Be right out."

She straightened her desk, gathered her purse and

closed her door behind her. "See ya later, Kath," she called to her sister as she headed to the front. She opened the door to the reception area, and there stood Officer Dave McCoy as she'd never seen him before. Laughing and relaxed with his head thrown back, he was joking with Trish, who was almost old enough to be his mother.

Maybe it was the related occupation that gave them common ground. Whatever it was, Heather had to admit the man was attractive when he smiled.

"What can I do for you, Officer? And if you want to change my mind, forget it. I'm not filing charges against the creeps."

His smile disappeared, but when Dave looked at Trish, he winked. "Is she *always* grumpy? Or is it me?"

"Not for me to say," replied the guard, her wide grin bright against her bronze complexion.

"Smart lady," said Heather as she studied the big cop. This casual behavior was not typical of Dave. He definitely wanted something from her. "I've got a class at the university in forty-five minutes. What's on your mind?"

He nodded at the exit. "Outside."

She went ahead of him through the door and down the two steps to the driveway. Then she turned to face him. And got a surprise. For a moment, he looked… uncertain. Worried. So *not* McCoy.

"Just spill it, Officer McCoy," she encouraged, as though speaking to a needy client.

"We have reason to believe there was a fourth man last night at the scene," he said quietly, not wasting any words. "We believe he's the brother of the suspect you brought down. So, until we learn more, I suggest you take precautions. No going out in that broken-down vehicle. No going out alone, day or night. No…"

She put up a hand. "Hold it. First, I don't take orders from anyone, cops included. Second, I'm not running away. Or hiding. There's only one way to take care of bullies, McCoy." She leaned forward and poked him in the chest. "You stand up to them."

He nodded. "A bully, however, is not a bullet. How do you stand up to one of those? For all we know, the brother could have followed us back to your house last night. Now, I probably would have noticed someone tailing me, but—

"And I trust your instincts, so we have no problem. Thanks for the warning. You did your job. And now, I'm off." She took three more steps.

"Not so fast."

Dave stood with his arms crossed over his chest.

His unblinking stare got her attention. "I'm telling you plain, Ms. Marshall. If you go out again without a partner, I'll have a conversation with the oil man."

He meant Mark, and she'd really hate for such a meeting to take place, but… "Do you think you can threaten me?" she asked, walking toward him. "Well, I won't be bullied, either, McCoy, so stay out of my business. Stay away from my family."

"Not a chance. You're a pain in my butt, but I'd rather see you alive than dead." He leaned toward her and spoke softly and slowly. "People in drug cartels do not play around. It's no game to them—it's big business."

Heather heard her own heartbeat in the silence that followed, but Dave wasn't finished. "Do you understand what I'm saying, Heather?"

"Yeah, I understand. I'm just the sandwich lady on the street. I am absolutely no threat to these guys. I didn't even press charges. You, however, did. So you'd better watch your own butt, Officer McCoy." She began walking.

"Our suspect cursed *la rubia,*" snapped McCoy, "the blonde. His pride took a hit, and now his emotion is clouding the business. His brother might act the same way. I don't like it."

"You worry too much, McCoy."

He was in her rearview mirror until she reached the interstate, the edge of his territory.

MARY BETH SHIFTED in bed and grimaced. No moaning allowed now that Neil and Megan were finally sleeping in their own beds after she'd carried them from hers. She would have let them stay with her the entire night, but the single bed couldn't accommodate three. Especially when Mom kept searching for a comfortable position.

She bit her lip to swallow another groan. She'd landed on her hip after Hank had thrown her against the stair railing last night, and she'd fallen down the complete flight. She thanked God it hadn't been worse. Hadn't prevented her from finally taking action. Megan and Neil, the most beautiful people in her life, had seen everything.

Tears welled out of her eyes as she lay on her back. She was a lousy mother. Children should be protected, not exposed to fear and ugliness. Oh, God, she should have taken the kids and left long ago before the abuse got worse. Before fear sucked the air from her lungs until she could barely breathe.

Not that she hadn't dreamed of escape. Even

prepared all their documents, had them packed and ready to go at any time. They were now in plastic Ziploc bags in her big tote. Birth certificates. Social Security cards. Marriage license. No restraining order, though. She hadn't had the guts. But she'd taken her journal. It wasn't a legal document, but a record she'd kept for her own sanity. To prove she was somebody. A flesh-and-blood somebody. With thoughts and feelings. To provide evidence if something happened to her.

After Hank left for work that morning, she knew the day had come. She didn't tell anyone. Not her friends. Not her parents. She'd left her car—so easily traceable. And she'd finally made the phone call.

Here they were at Welcome Home, safe for now in their own apartment on the second floor in the back. A full bathroom, two bedrooms and a living room. Tiny windows—locked, with curtains drawn. She'd been told that the first-floor units had no windows at all. Instead, colorful pictures hung everywhere, cheerful distractions. Flowers and ocean and sky. Freedom.

"Freedom." She tasted the syllables and thought about Neil and Megan. It was the best gift she could ever give her children.

CHAPTER THREE

"SOMEONE'S TAILING US."

Heather glanced into the rearview mirror of her sister's car. Tiffany was right. The guy she'd noticed earlier was still there, and he was definitely not McCoy. Too short behind the wheel. And too intense peering over it.

Her partner turned her head. "His headlights are blinking. Maybe he just wants to tell us we're leaking gasoline or something."

Heather glanced at the Welcome Home counselor. Tiffany wasn't naive. Just clueless about Monday night's incident, so she had no reason to be suspicious. "Maybe so," said Heather, "but he's been following us for a while, and he could have let us know at our last stop. There was plenty of room to pull over on that corner near Travis Park."

"Well..." Tiffany mused, "do you think he's hungry? Or maybe he's looking for action, which means he's got great taste!" Immediately, she made an exasperated sound. "But only an idiot tries to pick up women by scaring them to death on a highway."

"Tiff—I have no idea, but I'm going to try to lose him."

They'd just criss-crossed their way through neighborhood streets back to the service road. Now, instead of staying in the right lane near the stores, Heather worked her way left and entered the freeway at the last minute. There was a steady flow of traffic, and she wove in and out, matching her speed to the rest of the vehicles.

"Let's hope we're alone when we get off," said Tiffany.

Heather focused her attention on her driving. She stayed on for two exits and made a U-turn at the end of the next exit ramp, reversing directions. She turned into neighborhood streets, intent on keeping to her scheduled route, but caught herself checking her mirror often.

The next stops were uneventful except for the scarcity of teens. Without the white van as a beacon, the kids couldn't recognize her. By the end of the night, she and Tiffany had chatted with only seven youngsters. Heather hoped they'd spread the word about the change in vehicles until she got another van. "I've got too many sandwiches left over, guys," she'd told the last two boys.

By ten o'clock, she'd put her suspicions about being followed to rest, admitting that she'd allowed paranoia to take over on this quiet evening. All because of McCoy. Her mouth tightened. He'd done his duty, and she'd heard him out. But she didn't want to live her life always looking over her shoulder.

She headed home after dropping Tiffany off at her car, feeling much more relaxed. Until she got partway down her own block and saw headlights blinking in her rearview mirror. She shivered and tightened her hands on the wheel. Suddenly, she saw red, white and blue lights rotate on the roof of the car. Damn that McCoy! She'd kill him for scaring her to death. But when she pulled into her driveway and looked back, it was a female officer exiting the vehicle.

"Is everything all right, ma'am?" said the cop.

"Sure. I'm fine. Did McCoy quit?"

The woman laughed. "McCoy? Never. We're merely providing extra patrol for a while, Ms. Marshall."

Heather's eyes widened. "How did you know my name, Officer…?" She peered at the woman's badge.

"Hannity. Eve Hannity. I responded to your call Monday night. Glad to meet you."

And then Heather knew how it felt to be examined under a microscope. The cop seemed to memorize every cell of her body.

"Okay, Ms. Marshall. I'll wait until you're inside."

"Thanks, but...did you just happen to be here on my street right now? Or," she said with suspicion in her voice, "did McCoy put you up to it?"

The officer met her gaze. "I'm simply doing my job, trying to keep our citizens safe. Just like Officer McCoy. Good night."

Heather nodded, knowing she'd been dismissed. Eve Hannity might be an attractive female, but she was also a cop, trained to use authority. To maintain the almighty control. To Heather and every woman who lived at Welcome Home, control was a disease.

Heather entered the house she shared with her sister. A real home—where she was safe. Everyone should have a home like this. Especially kids.

Please be advised that the following projects have been funded for three years beginning January 1st in Houston, Texas:
YOUTHCRAFT
NEW HORIZONS
GIRLFRIENDS—A SHELTER FOR TEENAGE GIRLS

HEATHER STARED at the screen and gulped. "Do you see what I see?" she managed to whisper to Kathy. Her heart thumped so hard that her chest hurt. She rubbed her sweaty palms on her jeans.

"Yes, I see it," said Kathy, a huge grin spread across her face. "You did it, Heather!"

Heather's throat felt tight. She could scarcely believe she'd been given this chance. She studied the announcement again and blinked hard—very hard—but her tears fell anyway.

Kathy's arms felt warm and comforting around her. "Shh, Heather. It's time to celebrate. My goodness, that's twice this week. I'm not used to seeing you cry."

Heather held on to her sister. "Kath…I love working at Welcome Home, but a place for kids…God, I wish we'd had a place to go when we were growing up."

Kathy didn't reply for a long time. "Did you hate me for leaving you there, Heather?" she said finally. "Was I too selfish?"

Denial sprang to Heather's lips, but then she paused. Her sister wanted a considered response. "I would have taken that scholarship, too—anything to get out of there. So I didn't hate *you,* Kathy," she said slowly. "I hated *them.*" She squeezed her sister's hand. "I *never* hated you. I just wanted out. And here we are." Calm filled her as it did every time she remembered how far she'd come.

"We sure are two hardscrabble girls from west Texas," said Kathy. "Sometimes, I can't believe it myself." She turned to the computer again. "You have my full support on this project—as much help as I can provide."

"Thanks, Kathy. First up is finding my replacement at Welcome Home. I'll certainly help with the search and the transition."

But Kathy had gotten absorbed in what she was reading over Heather's shoulder. "Hold everything—did you see this? You got funded, but at fifty thousand dollars less than you'd asked for…you've got immediate access to monies for capital expenses, but…damn it! They didn't reduce the amount of services they want. They only reduced the funds. Now, how are you going to get this project going at full speed without that fifty thou?"

Heather stared at the announcement. "I guess the first thing I do is study the budget and see where I can save. Not with the kids…or staff…but maybe we can get the building up to code with volunteer help. I need to recruit someone who knows construction and who has a heart."

"And time," said Kathy. "Lots of people have good intentions. We need folks with the time and commitment to do it."

"We'll try to get materials donated." Heather sat back in her chair. "I didn't expect this money glitch. The start-up is going to be even harder than I thought."

"Heck, you've already come up with two ideas. This will be a piece of cake. In fact, it'll be as easy as shopping for your maid-of-honor dress this Saturday."

Heather groaned. "You're lucky I like Mark…."

Kathy hugged her tight. "I'm so proud of you, Heather. So glad we're family."

"Yeah. Me, too." But soon Kathy's life would be intertwined with Mark's. They'd be a new family, and Heather would be on her own again.

KATHY HAD BEEN WRONG. Shopping for a dress was not easy. It was as awful as Heather had expected. The bride hadn't been satisfied with anything Heather had tried on.

"Fine?" Kathy sounded outraged as Heather displayed the latest dress with a shrug. "We're looking for more than fine. When we see it, we'll know it."

And in the fourth dress shop, they had seen it. Deep purple, the silky material draped across one shoulder, leaving the other shoulder bare. The dress had sequins and beads scattered throughout and came with a matching wrap. When Heather saw herself in the full-length mirror, she understood what her more fashion-conscious sister was talking about. She, who applied makeup in less than a minute when she remembered, now saw that her blue eyes had taken on a deeper hue, the planes of her face were emphasized, her high cheekbones revealed. She twisted her long hair to the top of her head. "Oh, my."

"Like a queen. We're taking it. Can you measure and pin up her hem, please?" Kathy asked the salesclerk. "If you'd think about your social life more, Heather, you'd have a decent wardrobe. Jeans don't cut it everywhere." Kathy reached for her charge card.

"Wait a minute. You're not buying my dress." She looked at the saleswoman. "How much is this one?"

The woman showed her the tag. Heather gulped. "Neither one of us is buying this dress. Come on, Kath. I'm going to let you have more shopping fun. Let's go."

Her sister's eyes flashed. She stood rooted to the floor and smiled sweetly at the assistant. "Please get the tailor over here. My sister's got wedding jitters."

"But, Kathy, do you know how many sandwiches we could buy for that money? Or we could put it toward the new van…."

Kathy rolled her eyes. "You've got to draw boundaries, Heather. You are entitled to a personal life—without guilt. You look stunning in that dress, and you're getting it. Besides," she added, a smile lighting her face, "there will be an assortment of young eligible men at this affair, and I want them knocking each other down to get to you. I also want to show you off to Mark's family."

"I'm not looking…" Heather protested automatically. Then she paused. Mark's family? Maybe this wasn't about her love life at all.

"So, are you the one feeling jittery?"

Kathy shrugged.

"Kath—are you having second thoughts about Mark? If you are, hey, we can just call it off…."

But Kathy's swung her head back and forth. "No, no. Mark's wonderful. Truly wonderful. With a very big family who loves him very much. You know? Big." She spread her arms wide in emphasis. "But you're my family…the one that I can count on…and…and…"

Now Heather understood. "And you're nervous about Mark's family meeting our illustrious parents after all. Despite their two-year sobriety."

Her sister fingered the brocade of another dress hanging on the nearest rack. "What if…? What if they can't handle it? His family is generous—we're having an open bar. What if Daddy falls off the wagon and falls on his face while walking me down the aisle?"

"And you think I'm the one with the imagination," said Heather. "There's an easy fix. Just don't invite them."

Kathy shook her head quickly. "People deserve second chances."

Maybe other people. "You're right, of course," said Heather softly. She trusted her parents less than Kathy did. A lot less. If George and Jolene did anything—said anything—to ruin Kathy's wedding…

"Tell you what I'll do, Kath. Simply because you and Mark deserve a perfect day without any embarrassing scenes, I'll take responsibility for them. Don't give old George and Jolene a second thought. They're in my charge." She'd think up some kind of plan. Maybe hire someone to keep tabs on her dad—at least to share the chore.

"I know I'm worrying for nothing," said Kathy. "They're sober. It's a big wedding. They'll be on their best behavior."

Maybe. Maybe not. Heather couldn't vouch for her parents one way or the other. Although she'd spoken to her mother over the years, she hadn't visited Dry Creek since she'd boarded that bus a decade ago. Kathy and Mark had gone out there last year, so Heather figured her folks couldn't have been too bad. Mark had stuck around.

Her cell phone rang, but she knew better than to disturb the tailor who was pinning her dress. She gestured to Kathy who fished around in Heather's purse until she found the mobile. She said hello, listened for a moment, then smiled at Heather.

"It's Sara. She wants you at her birthday party tonight."

"Keep talking for a minute." The hem was fully tacked, and Heather stepped out of the gown, gave it to Kathy and quickly got back into her casual clothes. With one hand, she reached for the cell phone; the other hand lingered on the soft material in Kathy's arms. It really was a beautiful dress.

Sara didn't waste a word. "A personal appeal will do wonders for your cause. If you can touch their heartstrings, Heather, you'll raise more money than I can alone. Tell them about the kids…how it feels to be…powerless…."

Her voice trailed off, and Heather knew Sara was remembering Dry Creek. Sara was the one kid in that town who understood exactly how Heather and Kathy had grown up.

"You know what, Heather?" said Sara. "I think you ease my conscience about the money I earn, and that's why I'm glad to help out. Now, I'm going to give you a piece of advice about tonight. Wear something provocative to interest the men, but not too threatening to the women. If you make friends with both genders, you'll collect more green."

"Provocative? What are you talking about? I'll come after I feed some kids. Then I'll make my speech and get the heck out of there."

She disconnected the call, Sara's laughter still ringing in her ears.

She had to figure a way to get people to part with their hard-earned money. Without being provocative.

"YOUR HEATHER can sure be a handful."

Not exactly the greeting Dave had expected when he arrived at Eve's house early Saturday evening. "Here's dessert," he replied, handing her a gallon of ice cream.

"Thanks. Want to cool off with it now?" She

grinned way up into his face from her five-foot-two vantage point, before leading him into the kitchen where Larry was basting a huge rack of ribs, and a petite blonde was tossing potato salad.

"You know Larry, my husband. And this is my sister, Lisa," said Eve. "Direct from New Yawk."

Dave shook hands with the man and smiled at the woman, who was still busy with the food. "Hey, Lisa from New Yawk. Welcome to Texas."

Eve hadn't lied. Her sister was a blond, blue-eyed cutie. Probably easier to deal with than another blonde he knew.

"Glad to be here," said Lisa. "I don't get to visit family nearly often enough."

Dave automatically scanned for details. Her eyes were shadowed, tinged with sadness.

"We're trying to convince her to move here," said Eve. "She's burned out on her job. She's alone up north, and I'm alone here. Well—" she glanced at her husband "—not exactly alone…but our folks are gone. So, why not?" She hooked her arm through Dave's. "But she's being stubborn. Like the Marshall woman. Now, why can't they all be like me? Reasonable. Fair."

Dave was still chuckling when he stepped outside

to the patio. He heard Larry cracking up in the background. Heard Lisa's softer laugh joining in. Sometimes, he wished he'd had a brother or sister. Maybe he'd take his mom to breakfast tomorrow. Catch up with his dad in the afternoon. He sighed. Too bad their marriage couldn't have worked out.

"Hey, McCoy," called Jazzman. "I've got more info about our big adventure this week with Ms. Marshall…turns out that two of the guys are undocumented. The DHS is dealing with them. Out of our hair. But the other one…a real upstanding citizen. He'll get bail, mark my words."

"I heard," said Dave. "And naturally, he's the one Heather brought down."

Jazzman's eyebrows rose. "Heather, is it?"

"Knock it off."

"Yes, sir. Sergeant, sir. Yes, sir." Jazzman saluted.

Dave had to laugh.

New people kept arriving during the next hour; the patio filled up. Sure they talked shop, but they also caught up on Houston politics, and on one another's families. Dave learned that Eve's sister worked for Children's Protective Services, had a humongous caseload, which was why she was exhausted. He studied the pictures of his friends' kids. Too long between gatherings, thought Dave. In this informal atmosphere, with these guys, he could just be himself. No putting on a show face as he had to on duty. “You throw a nice party, Hannitys.”

The loud ring of the kitchen phone prevented Eve from responding. A dozen pair of eyes followed her as she ran to answer it.

When Eve appeared in the doorway, her gaze deliberately fell on him.

“That was Powers,” Yorkie began. “The karate kid’s car was hit...with her in it. She’s fine, but it was a deliberate action.”

Dave jumped up, leaped the backyard fence and ran down the driveway. Then he ran back. “Where the hell is she?”

“The same place as last time. Scene of the original crime.”

Dave dashed toward his car, but heard Eve say loud enough for him to hear, “Men. He’s in love with a clueless sitting duck. And doesn’t even know it.”

“She’s not clueless,” he yelled. “Just stubborn. And it’s because of the kids. And I’m not...” He shut up. No one could hear him flying down the block in his car.

TEN MINUTES LATER, he stared at a Heather Marshall he'd never seen before. Her long hair tousled, she was wearing a sleeveless black blouse with black slacks, and high-heeled black sandals. Hot pink on her toes, fingernails and lips. She was stunning.

Powers had waited, and there were a couple of teenage girls around, too.

Where was she going dressed like that? Was there a guy in her life?

"We really…have to stop meeting like this," she said softly before pressing her lips together. He knew bravura when he saw it. The woman was scared. Finally.

He didn't move except to hold out his hand. She took it, and somehow wound up leaning against him, his arms around her. He inhaled her scent, so light and delicate, and felt her warmth.

"I got frightened because it was the same man."

Dave stiffened. He started scanning the area one section at a time. "I've explained to Ms. Marshall that all three are still in jail," Powers jumped in. His eyes met Dave's, a question in them.

"She knows about the brother," said Dave. "I told her."

Heather stepped back. "He followed me Wednesday night…I'm almost positive."

Out alone again? And why didn't she mention the incident to him? She held her hand up before Dave could say anything. "I had a partner with me, Officer McCoy. Tiffany Peters, one of my staff at the shelter. Ask her if you don't believe me."

"You're not a liar. You're as up-front as they get. I do know that much."

She turned to Officer Powers. "Thank you very much. I'm glad you were nearby. But I'm all right now. And I've got to talk to these kids." She flashed a megawatt smile at the girls and waved them closer. "Come on. I've got great news. Just found out."

Dave listened as she explained about Girlfriends—a shelter for teenage girls. So, he'd have another group to watch out for in his district.

"But if you want to get off the streets now, how about checking out the Youth Center?" Heather said.

"No way, Ms. Heather. Brenda's not even there anymore. And I'm not going, neither."

"Where *is* Brenda?"

The girl shrugged. "Hangin' somewhere, I guess. She said they had too many rules. And they wanted to call her folks or CPS. She just booked outta there."

Dave's brain started clicking. Brenda had been

one of the girls involved in Monday night's incident. One girl had called her parents, but Brenda had chosen the Youth Center. Evidently not for long. Maybe Heather was on the right track opening a new place for the girls.

Powers had another call on the radio and had to leave. Dave looked at Heather. "How about feeding these kids, and I'll follow you home?"

"Home? Oh, my goodness. I almost forgot where I was going."

This should be interesting, but he'd bet no guy was involved. She wouldn't have forgotten about a lover, no matter what.

"I'm out to raise money."

"Ah. You're going to play Robin Hood, aren't you? You're going to hit on the rich for your shelters—maybe the River Oaks crowd," he said.

She smiled. "Not exactly River Oaks, but you're on the right track. My friend Sara is rich, and her friends have more. And I want their donations. So, I'm trying to fit in tonight at Sara's birthday party. Kathy made me dress up. I even have a script."

He shook his head. "Oh, you'll fit in all right. And the men will definitely see you…."

"I hope not," she said. "I want their vision blurred

by a few teardrops. My goal is to unplug their ducts, so they'll open their wallets."

"Hope you brought a lot of soft soap," he said. "You'll need it."

"You think I can't be charming?"

Charming like a bulldog. He opened the passenger door of his pickup. "Get in, and we'll find out. We'll get your sister's car later." This was not exactly the evening he'd had in mind.

"I can make it on my own," she said. "I'm okay now."

"Look, Ms. Marshall, if you don't want to ride with me, that's fine. But I'm still going to follow you and make sure you get where you're going in one piece."

"But you're not even on duty," she protested.

"This is still my case report. But you're right about tonight—I'm off duty. And that's why you're going to repay me by going to Eve Hannity's house after you make your money pitch. My buddies and I were gathering there to set up some study sessions for the sergeant's exam. And I still aim to do that."

So what if he didn't sound very chivalrous. Heather Marshall was taking a chunk out of his evening, and lately a chunk out of his life. Besides, he'd been enjoying himself at Eve's...but now another idea struck him. A more important one.

The party offered a great opportunity for his friends to ID Heather. She'd get extra protection and not even realize it.

CHAPTER FOUR

SARA PATTERSON had the makings of a cop. When Heather had introduced her girlfriend to Dave, they'd exchanged head-to-toe detailed examinations, not polite glances. Her handshake was all business, too, and then she snaked her arm around Heather's waist protectively. And after a minute of her clever questions, he heartily approved of Sara Patterson.

"Happy Birthday," said Dave, loudly over the throbbing music and the sound of people dancing on the packed dance floor. It was amazing that the private room of Stepping Out, one of Houston's most popular clubs, could hold this many bodies.

The redhead's green eyes sparkled as brightly as the silver dress she wore. But she kept her arm around Heather. "Thanks. I'm making up for all the birthdays I never celebrated as a kid."

"Except kids get to keep their presents."

"If they have loving parents. Other kids grow up fast."

The two women eyed each other in silent communication. These two had a special rapport—they shared something in common—but he didn't know exactly what. Not yet.

Then Heather stepped away from her friend. "We're sort of on a schedule tonight, Sara. McCoy…uh, I mean Dave is expected at another party."

Sara nodded toward a quieter corner. Dave and Heather both followed her. "I just want to make sure you know he's carrying."

Dave winced. Evidently, his cotton button-down shirt wasn't doing the job. Heather stared blankly at her friend.

"A weapon, Heather. A gun," Sara explained.

"Oh, that." Heather waved the concern away. "He's a cop, Sara. HPD." She shrugged with open hands in that "what can you do?" kind of way.

Sara's eyes widened. No games, no teasing. "You're going out with a cop?" Substitute Darth Vader for cop and the horror would be equal. "No offense—personally," she added.

Yeah. Right. "None taken." He put on his cop face. Cool. Expressionless. Controlled. The sooner

Heather did her appeal, the better. Spending an unexpected evening with Heather was one thing, but wasting an evening with "attitude" was something else. He could've been back at Yorkie's place with his buds really enjoying himself.

"Relax, Sara," replied Heather. "We're not dating. My car was hit. He's doing me a favor. He's on the beat at Welcome Home."

Sara's visible relief would've been perfect on a sitcom, but Dave found nothing funny about it. So be it. People had all kinds of attitudes about the police, and at least Sara was open about her feelings. Her second welcome on Heather's behalf was warm and genuine. And that was a plus in Dave's book. He liked the idea of Heather having loyal friends.

Sara danced her way toward the deejay and when the current song ended, she took the microphone.

"Welcome to my birthday bash. Hope you're all having a great time."

Shouts and whistles from the guests.

"All right! I promise you there's plenty more party to come. But now, it's time to pay back. Or pay forward. However you like to think about it." She introduced Heather as the lady who spends her evenings bringing food and clothing to runaway kids. Then Heather took the floor.

Unexpectedly, Dave felt his heart begin to pound as he waited for Heather to begin. The woman worked so hard at a job that would never make her wealthy—just like his job—and he wanted her to succeed. More importantly, a new van would keep her safe. And give him peace of mind.

The crowd quieted down. Heather took the microphone from Sara.

"Thank you for allowing me to tell a story or two about the kids I work with. The kids are real, and their stories are true. One night last year, when I was out in my van, a young girl showed up at one of my usual stops. She was alone. A pretty girl. Maybe too pretty, with her curly blond hair and deep blue eyes. She walked slowly toward me, then hesitated, as if deciding whether to speak, whether to trust me. But I held out a bunch of sandwiches, and she was hungry. Now, I've gone through this same scenario many times with many children. But I've never forgotten the first words that particular fifteen-year-old said to me."

Heather paused, and the room was silent. "'It's just me and God against the world. And sometimes, it's just me.'"

As Dave watched her, Heather stopped for a moment and scanned the crowd before she picked up her story. "The world, ladies and gentlemen, is a very big place. And very, very scary to a child who's been abused from the time she can remember. In this case by her father and an uncle. Her bruises weren't always hidden, but no one intervened. No one helped her. So she ran away."

Some of the guests were already reaching for their wallets.

"I was able to help because I was there. But my van is beyond repair—over ten years old now and off the road."

Questions came flying from the audience. "Where do you take the kids? What happened to that girl? Is Houston a Mecca for runaways? Do the police get involved?"

Dave listened to her answers. And after four years on the beat, realized that besides Heather's passion for the kids and disregard for herself, she was also rational and clearly intelligent. He'd never have guessed it from the rash acts he'd seen while on duty. She was confident in public speaking, too. Around the room, everyone was writing a check. And Dave reached into his own back pocket.

But he'd bet his last gallon of gas, that his next interaction with Heather Marshall would be more trouble.

"OH, MY GOD. I'm so lucky Sara offered to handle all the contributions until next week. I didn't even bring a bank deposit bag with me. Dave, did you see how so many folks volunteered to help with Girlfriends? We'll be rolling right along with the new facility…." Heather glanced at Dave behind the wheel of his pickup. "I'm babbling, aren't I?"

He honest-to-goodness smiled when he turned to her. And she caught her breath. Handsome, yes. But his approval stunned her. In four years, this was the first time. Maybe he didn't think she was such a ditz.

"Babble all you want," he said. "You did a terrific job up there. Knocked me out, actually."

"Knocked myself out, too. I was a nervous wreck. I hate the public speaking stuff. Kathy's better at it. Much more eloquent."

"She couldn't have done any better than you did tonight," said Dave. "Let's see. You managed to get hours of free legal services from the lawyers, a rock-bottom wholesale price for a van, and numerous hours of sweat equity for the new building. I'd say you batted a thousand."

She took a deep breath. "Wow, the great Dave McCoy thinks I did something right for a change."

He was silent. When Heather stared at him in surprise, his eyes were strictly on the road, his mouth tight.

"We're almost at Eve and Larry's house," he said. "No personal comments are necessary."

He wasn't getting his way tonight. "Don't tell me I've insulted you, Officer McCoy! After all the times you've bullied me and talked to me like I was an idiot, who would have thought you could be so sensitive?"

"I'm not," he replied quickly. "And I've never called you an idiot."

"Don't get technical. You've made me feel like one and I didn't like it."

He pulled up along the curb and shut off the ignition. In the light of a streetlamp, Heather saw a tic start to throb under his jaw.

"If the great Dave McCoy thinks you've done something 'right' for a *change*," Dave said, "then explain what you've been doing for the last four years."

She paused with her fingers on the door handle and looked him squarely in the eyes. "My job, McCoy. I've been doing my job."

They both got out of the cab, their doors slamming in unison.

Dave walked around the truck and led Heather up the driveway to the Hannitys' backyard. "Relax," he said, "and try to enjoy yourself. These are the folks who've saved your butt a time or two."

"And I'm grateful that they do their *job* so well."

He threw up his hands. "Do you always need to have the last word?"

"Only when I'm right."

"You *always* think you're right."

Heather didn't reply. She needed to mull that statement over.

Officer Hannity stuck her head out the door, a big smile of welcome on her face. "Come on in. We're all in the family room. Ms. Marshall, I'm glad to see you're in one piece. Everything okay?" she asked Dave as she let them in.

"Her sister's car is banged up a bit. I'll fill ya'll in later."

Eve nodded. "We saved some burgers and dogs for you. There's plenty for two."

Heather's stomach rumbled in reply, and Eve chuckled. "Introduce her around, Dave, while I put the food on the grill."

And suddenly Heather found herself in the midst of law enforcement. A whole roomful. And each person greeted her in that annoying way she was getting used to. As if she was a specimen on a petri dish. For some reason, Dave made sure she either shook hands or spoke to every single officer in the room. Unexpectedly, the introductions exhausted her. She would have preferred a general, "Hi, y'all."

She found a seat, but had a hard time relaxing. Being herself. She listened to them swap stories, similar to the ones her father had told. Handling this perp and that offender. Maybe they were releasing tension. Maybe they needed the comradery of others in the same job. She felt as if she was suffocating.

Dave walked over. "Something wrong, Heather? The hamburgers are just about ready. So, don't go fainting again."

She smiled in acknowledgment, wondering if he'd ever forget that one time in the parking lot. And also wondering how he knew she felt unsettled. "It's not that…." Her voice trailed off.

"Then what?"

She stood and turned her back on the others. "It's just occurred to me," she whispered, "that I could be sitting in a room with about twenty people who are carrying. That's twenty loaded guns in one room." She gulped. "That's a lot of guns." And now he'd probably laugh at her and revert to thinking she didn't have a brain in her head.

"You're absolutely right," he said quietly. "But no one here thinks of a weapon as a toy. Rather, it's a piece of equipment we need for the job. We don't show our weapons off, we don't leave them lying around, we don't play with them. We follow all the safety rules. And besides," he added, "we're the good guys."

Not all of you. She returned a brief smile before Mary Beth sprang to her mind. "I'll take your word for this crowd. But no police force is perfect."

"Point taken. And just in time. Eve's waving us over."

Heather watched Dave's burgers disappear in minutes. She'd barely downed a few bites of hers. "Your food bill must be astronomical."

He chuckled. "My mom always said I had a hollow leg. Still does, actually. I take her out to dinner quite often to make up for the cost of my teenage years, but I think she prefers inviting me over and cooking."

"With your appetite—it's a lot cheaper at home."

"That's exactly what she says."

"So, how does your mom feel about her son being one of Houston's Finest?"

Silence. "Now that's a very interesting question," Dave finally replied. "And the answer is, I don't know."

And that was a very interesting answer as far as Heather was concerned.

THEY REJOINED THE GROUP in the family room and within minutes, Heather was able to single out the guests who were not part of the brotherhood. The spouses, male and female. And Eve's sister, Lisa Connors, who was now crossing the room to her.

"I hope I'm not intruding," she began, looking first at Dave, then at Heather. "I promised Eve I'd chat with you about working in Houston."

"I'm not a cop," replied Heather quickly.

Lisa grinned. "A blind man could see that."

"Lisa's a social worker like you," said Dave, "and Eve's suggesting that she relocate to Houston." He glanced over at his coworker. "Let's say Eve is pushing the idea."

"And she can be very persuasive…but…I'm starting to think it's not a bad idea. She's my only family."

Lisa's situation was similar to hers and Kathy's,

thought Heather. "I've got a sister, too," she said, "and I'm glad we're both in Houston." She indicated the seat next to her, and Lisa sat down.

Heather had a new facility to staff and her old job to fill. She focused only on Lisa and was glad when Dave left them to chat with his friends and set up that study schedule.

But ten minutes later, Dave was back. "Why don't you tell everyone about the new place you're building? Maybe you'll get some volunteers."

She had no intention of spending long working days with a bunch of cops who were used to taking charge and giving orders. But Dave was waiting, his expression eager. "I guess they'll find out anyway, so I'll announce it," she replied.

"All right," he said, giving her a thumbs-up. "Hey, guys. Heather's got some news for the north side of the Katy."

Instantly, all eyes were on her, almost like a replay of her earlier presentation to Sara's friends. The two groups, however, could not have been more disparate. She remained seated, more informal than when she presented to the other group. And as she told Officer Hannity's guests about Girlfriends, Heather realized that her goals were different with this crowd. She needed to inform. Educate. And help them to help her. No fund-raising.

"We'll be opening in January. I'll be able to take up to twenty girls, all minors. We'll integrate them into the public schools if possible. If not, we have funding for a tutor. But first we'll tackle the hierarchy of needs—food, clothing, shelter."

"Referrals from…?"

"Everywhere…and I'll also take the girls right from the streets. I'm still doing mobile outreach."

She couldn't tell if the buzz around the room was approval or not.

When Heather stood up, the room quieted. "A youngster who's run away," she began, "has taken the most desperate step a child can take. She's shouting for help. And *someone has got to hear her.*" She paused to let the words sink in. "Will you help me to help them?"

Absolute silence. Then one after another, they started clapping. The room rang with their cheers. She hadn't expected it and was almost shocked. Was her mind that closed toward police officers? Were the cops actually her allies? She glanced at Dave. He led the applause.

Heather felt the heat rise to her face and quickly

looked away. As she sat down again, she listened to the group's remarks.

"It's amazing someone still wants to save the world."

"A nice change after dealing with scum all day."

"I like the part about helping when they're still young."

"Amen, brother."

"And speaking of brothers," said one of the guests, "I heard through the grapevine that there's a beat cop across town who's filed missing persons on his wife and two kids. Says she's been clinically depressed. Thinks she might hurt herself and the kids. Even tried to get an APB out on her."

"An APB? Will never happen. Unless the women's a dangerous criminal. And I'll bet she has no record. What's her name?"

From flaming heat to icy cold, Heather held her breath and stared into her lap. Mary Beth Landers. Had to be. Heather could hear her own heartbeat.

"Last name of Landers. Officer Hank Landers."

Her hands tightened into fists. *Keep listening.*

"He's filed a missing person, huh?" someone said. "Which means he's already checked the local hospitals and found nothing."

"Which might also mean," inserted Lisa Connors, looking around the room, "that the woman made a rational decision to leave, and he'll never find any reports at local agencies. So, bravo to her."

Heather snapped to attention and stared at the woman.

"Aw, Yorkie. Your sister thinks we're pigs."

"No. No, I don't," replied Lisa. "But I've walked in her shoes—not with kids thankfully. Believe me, you're not all wonderful to live with." She paused for a moment. "But the way I figure it, I picked the rotten apple in the barrel. I'm just thankful I never married him."

"When did all this happen? Why didn't you tell me?" asked Eve, walking quickly toward her sister.

Lisa tilted her head. "Because you would have been on the next plane, and I didn't want a shoot-out on Broadway."

"Broadway? So, the SOB works the Midtown precinct? I know people there...."

"Eve!"

The policewoman turned to her husband. "What?"

"You're missing the point. It's over. Lisa handled it. Stop playing bossy big sister, or you'll lose her."

That silenced the woman. She smiled at her

husband. "That's why I married you, Larry. You keep me sane."

"But who keeps me sane?" he asked with a wink.

Eve bestowed a big lover's kiss right on Larry's mouth in front of everyone. "I do."

A new barrage of cheers and whistles signaled the end of the party. Guests began to take off.

Heather yawned as she and Dave walked to his truck.

"Tired?" he asked.

"What a night. I feel like I've both performed in and attended a play in about seventeen acts."

He opened the door for her and helped her in. "Those shoes aren't made for pickups, uh, no pun intended."

She glanced at her high-heeled sandals. The sexy choice. "No offense taken. My feet are killing me. I'm wearing a uniform."

"Nice uniform you've got there." He shut her door. A minute later, he pulled away from the curb. "So, when did Mrs. Landers and her kids show up at the shelter?"

And every friendly thought she'd started to have about McCoy vanished.

IT WAS AFTER MIDNIGHT when Heather pulled Kathy's car into the driveway. And she was happy to have had some time alone in the vehicle, away from McCoy. She hadn't confirmed Mary Beth's presence at Welcome Home. But McCoy knew. Said her gestures and expressions had given her away. Looking down. Avoiding his glance. She was no actress, so his observations were probably true. Which was too bad.

"And it's so Heather," he'd said with an exaggerated sigh. "Always getting the tough cases."

She could handle tough cases. She wasn't sure about tough cops. And more than that, she wasn't sure where McCoy's loyalty rested—with the cop or with the cop's victims. Could he possibly have twenty-twenty vision in this?

She parked the car and walked to McCoy's truck at the curb to say good-night. But the cop was standing beside a silent vehicle, and Heather was surprised. She was home safely now, and he could leave.

"Thanks a lot, McCoy. I appreciate the help, the ride. Everything. But you can get going now."

"After you tell me if Kathy's home," he said.

"Nope. They're with Mark's family this weekend in the hill country."

"Then I'm not leaving until I check it out," he said, nodding toward the house.

"I locked it before I left."

"Good. Come on." Heather shrugged, then led him inside. "Stay here," he ordered, "right by the doorway."

"Fine," she said, deciding to humor him. She watched him pull back the drapes in the living room, right off the entry hall. The dining room on the opposite side was empty. She could see that for herself. The house only had three bedrooms. No big family room, no fancy granite countertops to show off, just a simple home, comfortable enough for the two sisters, in a working-class neighborhood. There was certainly nothing to draw a burglar here.

Heather removed the killer shoes, leaned against the wall and waited, as she imagined his actions in each room to be like every cop's in every police show she'd ever seen. He took longer than she'd thought.

"The locks on your bedroom windows stink," he said, replacing his weapon in its holster. "And you don't even have an alarm system. A baby crook could break in here without a problem."

"We don't own the house. We rent it."

"Tell your landlord that an alarm system is a home improvement, and he'll save on his insurance."

She saluted. "Yes, sir."

He glared at her. "Not funny."

"I'm tired, McCoy. Go home."

"I guess long nights don't agree with you. Lock up after me."

He stepped outside, and she turned the tumblers. Then heard him call, "Good girl."

As though she were ten years old. She listened to his truck engine start up, the noise diminishing as he drove away. Finally, she could relax. She picked up her shoes and walked down the hall to her bedroom, humming under her breath. When she glanced at herself in the mirror, she paused. She looked…passable. Maybe more than passable. Actually a bit sophisticated with her hair curly and wild and some blush on her cheeks.

A fast rap on the front door interrupted her musings. What could McCoy want now? She ran down the hallway, pulled the door open and found herself staring into the muzzle of a gun. And it wasn't McCoy's.

DAVE PULLED AWAY from Heather's house and started cruising the streets. Funny how wide-awake he felt when exchanging words with Heather should have wiped him out. She both captivated and exasperated him. He couldn't quite determine how to deal with her yet. But he would.

He drove up and down neighborhood streets,

hoping to unwind before going home. He'd rather stay out late and drive than toss and turn before he was ready to sleep. He made his way past the women's shelter, then zigzagged through his territory.

The streets were quiet, and a few minutes later, he yawned. Twice. His signal to head home. Instinctively, he chose Heather's block to access the freeway, laughing at himself. When he saw the panel truck in front of her house, however, his humor fled. He squeezed his brakes as he approached. Where the hell did that truck come from? And why was it parked in front of Heather's door when there were plenty of other spots on the block? He'd only been gone a little while, and he didn't like coincidences.

He pulled in front of the truck, cut his engine and climbed out. Then he drew his gun. Sliding into the shadows, he made his way to the front door and turned the knob. The door swung open revealing a dark empty hallway. He sidled along the wall leading to the back of the house, halting at the sound of voices. A man's low one, and Heather's shaky one—coming from her bedroom at the end of the corridor on the right. He'd been in it earlier.

He approached silently in the dark. The bedroom door was partly open. A man stood in profile, a gun drawn on Heather. In a tone that belonged to a lover, soft words rolled out of his mouth.

"Your boyfriend, the cop, pressed charges on my family, no? A real hero. And payback is—how you say—a real…bitch." He shrugged his shoulders, but a hungry grin crossed his face. "First, *puta,* you will take off the sexy blouse…and show me those beautiful round treasures." He gestured impatiently with the weapon. "Now!"

"I'm not a whore…."

"Do it!" the perp ordered sharply, his gun steady, pointing at Heather. "I'm going to have what my brother didn't," he added, "and then, *puta,* we take a little trip, and the boyfriend will never find you…."

"I don't think so," said Dave.

The man whirled, his weapon discharging.

"Get down," yelled Dave, as he shot the gun out of the guy's hand. Blood spurted, but the perp came charging at Dave like a young bull elephant. The man used his whole body, and his powerful impact jarred the cop, whose gun hit the floor. Dave kicked it across the room as his fist connected with the man's cheek. He fought the perp punch by punch, connecting with his gut, then his nose. It felt great to release.

Not so great to receive. But the piece of turd wasn't going to hurt Heather.

He grabbed the man around his chest trying for a full-body hold. But the guy fought back. His arms and legs struck like pistons. He kneed Dave near his groin, and Dave flung his whole weight against him. They both twisted off balance and hit the floor, Dave underneath.

From his position on the ground, Dave saw Heather approach. She held something over her head. *No!* He tried to shout, "Get out of here." But his breath was gone, his words soft.

As he watched, her eyes widened. She'd heard him, and for a second, he hoped she'd leave the place. Then she smashed the perp over the back of his head—not once, but twice—with a metal pole. The man went limp, a heavy deadweight.

"Vacuum cleaner," Heather whispered.

Dave pushed the man off, and looked at Heather. "Crazy woman. Got any panty hose?"

She dropped the vacuum, nodded and disappeared. Dave retrieved both weapons.

"Kathy's," she said, handing him the nylon hose a moment later. While he tied the man's wrists behind his back, Heather got the portable phone from the kitchen. Her hands began to shake, and Dave grabbed the receiver.

"You would have been better off kicking the guts out of this one, too," he murmured.

She smiled briefly, and he almost collapsed with relief. Until he saw her tears. Instantly, he felt like beating the bastard to a spongy blob. He reached out and drew her close. When she leaned into him, he wanted to tuck her away.

Then he called 911. This emergency stuff was getting to be a habit he wanted to break.

CHAPTER FIVE

"I THOUGHT IT WAS YOU. I thought it was you." She wanted to explain. Wanted Dave to believe her. His friends, too. Officer Powers still stood in the hallway after two other cops had taken the creep away.

"Do you need any medical attention?" asked Powers in a gentle voice, his gaze passing from Heather to Dave, whose arm was still around her.

"No," replied Heather. "I'm fine, I'm really fine. I just need a minute. You understand why I opened the door, don't you? I thought it was McCoy." She was repeating herself, and she pressed her lips together to keep quiet.

"Look at Dave's bruises. It's Dave who needs medical help. His cheek is swelling. I'll get an ice pack right now…." She ran to the kitchen, the men right behind her.

She took an ice tray out of the old freezer and smashed it against the side of the sink. Oh, that felt good. She grabbed another tray. And smashed it on top of the first. Better. After filling a plastic bag with cubes, she wrapped it with a paper towel and placed it carefully against Dave's cheek. "Hold it there." She would have held it for him, but she had too much energy to stand still. Maybe adrenaline. Maybe aftershock. She could've run a marathon. She wanted to calm her mind, calm her body. No more being a victim. She knew exactly what she had to do.

She explained to the two that she needed to be alone, thanked them again and left Dave in the kitchen. In the third bedroom, she started working out on the heavy bag she'd installed when she and Kathy had leased the house. She found it hard to focus at first, and her technique was sloppy. Knees, elbows, feet. Some shadowboxing. Slower, concentrate. Take your time, build your strength. Breathe. She managed to get into the zone, slowly bringing everything she'd learned about the discipline into this practice session.

Dave watched Heather from the bedroom door after Powers left. He knew she was oblivious to him, and it didn't matter. He couldn't stop staring. Heather Ann Marshall worked the bag with an expertise beyond anyone he'd ever seen. If she weren't a black belt kickboxer, she was close. He replayed the first encounter they'd had with the gang. How she'd kicked the perp with precision and took him out of the game. She'd kicked the knives away. And how she'd gotten in the perp's face, screaming about her kids. Fearless. And now he knew why.

Tonight, however, had been different. A loaded gun had been pointed directly at her.

Finally, she paused, hugged the bag and slowly slid to the floor.

"All finished?" he asked softly.

She looked up at him through long lashes and smiled. And his heart pounded a syncopated beat. He caught his breath as he stared at her. Despite the sweat and the dark smudges on her cheeks where her makeup had run, she looked beautiful. Were his friends right? Eve had said he was in love with a sitting duck.

"I'm staying the night," he said. "Or what's left of it."

"Good."

Good, she had company? Or good that company was him?

"I need a shower," she said, slowly rising to her feet. "I stink."

He hadn't noticed.

She looked down at herself. "This is what I get for dressing up…."

"The guy's a sicko, Heather. You didn't provoke anything."

"Of course not," she replied immediately. "I know that." She patted his arm. "It's just that now I've ruined this fancy silk outfit."

"I'll buy you another one." As if silk clothing mattered more than her life.

"No, no, Dave. It wasn't your fault. You don't owe me anything."

That wasn't what he'd meant at all. "I liked seeing you all dressed up. You looked very pretty."

She laughed. "You'll have to use your memory. Tomorrow it's back to jeans and running shoes. Thank God."

He followed her to the front of the house. Almost bumped into her when she froze in the hall near the kitchen. She stared at the front door. "Did you lock it?" she whispered.

And then he knew the evening's aftermath was far from over. "Sure did. Both tumblers. But you should have a keyed entry. Better yet, you need an alarm system."

She nodded. "Okay."

No argument. No lip. Her experience was beginning to take root. It had been real.

"There might be a beer in the fridge," said Heather. "And there's plenty of soft drinks. Help yourself. I'm cleaning up." She left him in the kitchen.

Thirty minutes later, after soaking his hands in icy water and laying the ice pack on his face for as long as he could stand it, Dave still waited for her to reappear.

THE HOT WATER CLEANED HER on the outside and warmed her on the inside. She felt wonderful. No more shivering at all. She was safe in her own house with…Dave McCoy, a cop. Another shiver ran through her. Not fear this time, but excitement, which surprised her. Maybe the cop shouldn't stay.

A loud rapping penetrated the sound of the water. "Heather. Are you okay in there? It's been a half hour."

"I'm fine. Coming right out." She dried off in a hurry, put on an oversize tee and shorts, and combed her wet hair just enough to take out the knots.

She walked into the kitchen, and Dave rose from his chair, his eyes filled with warmth and concern and…maybe something more…for her. And every thought she'd had about sending him away flew out of her head.

Before her stood not a cop. Not Officer Dave McCoy. But simply a man. A man who was looking at her now as though she were the last piece of chocolate on the plate.

"Dave...?" She tasted his name, rolled it on her tongue and slowly reached her hand toward him.

"Yes." He opened his arms, and she stepped inside.

"I was scared," she murmured against his chest. The admission pained her.

"I know."

"He would've...would've...taken me...and, and..."

"But he didn't. And he can't. He's not going anywhere for a long time. You're safe."

"Good grief. That's what I tell my clients at Welcome Home. 'You're safe.' Just what you're telling me."

His arms tightened around her. "They need to hear it...."

Just as she needed to. "They need to believe it. That's the difference." She moved out of his arms, stepped around him, then walked to the door and examined the locks. "I'm...I'm just making sure."

"Take your time. Do whatever helps you." His voice was gentle, and his movements quiet, small. Nonthreatening. Reassuring.

"Are you sure you can stay?"

"Absolutely. Heather…there's nowhere else I'd rather be."

Her name was a caress. "Then, would you mind just holding me?"

His mouth curved into a smile. "I think I can handle that."

She nodded at the couch. "We could stay near the front of the house and hear anyone who tries to come in."

"Yeah," he whispered, pulling her into his arms again. "We could do that." He tipped her chin up. "I like looking at you."

And she liked being in his arms. "Would you mind," she whispered, caressing his cheek, "one little kiss?"

His lips had barely skimmed hers, when she ignited. She kissed him back, hard. She needed speed and heat. She needed to feel alive. Heather set the pace.

In the end, they didn't even make it to the couch.

HE AWOKE TO SUNSHINE streaming through the window. His body ached, and there was no sign of Heather. *Brace yourself, McCoy. It's the morning after, so what do you expect?* He slowly got to his feet and stretched, then winced. He needed a hot shower.

"Good morning."

Heather stood at the entry to the living room, neat, clean and dressed in her usual jeans and a short-sleeved jersey. He examined her features one by one: eyes were clear, skin tone normal and her mouth...well, her mouth looked delicious enough to nibble.

"Good morning," he replied, his voice rusty. He coughed.

"I found a new toothbrush for you." She nodded toward the bathroom. "Go ahead. Take your time. I'll make breakfast."

She sounded cheerful enough, but in his experience, women were hard to predict. He'd follow her lead in this, too.

When he emerged from the bathroom feeling more human, the tantalizing breakfast aromas led him right to the kitchen. The table was set for two. A big frying pan had a mess of eggs, onions and green peppers in it, and the fragrance of freshly perked coffee had him salivating.

"We need to talk."

Just as he'd predicted. Morning-after regrets. "Mind if I have my coffee first?" he asked, trying to brace himself for the worst.

"Of course not. Here, I'll pour it." She handed him

an almost-full mug, retrieved a carton of milk from the refrigerator and gave it to him. She poured a second mug for herself and raised it in a toast as though it were a glass of champagne. "To life," she said before taking a sip.

"Always a good choice." And very appropriate today. Now, he knew where their conversation was heading. He swallowed once, then again, and enjoyed the liquid heat coursing through his body. He took the two full plates she handed him and set them on the table. Waited for her to get the toast and sit down.

"Smells delicious," he said. "I'm impressed. Another one of your hidden talents?"

Her head snapped up. "What do you mean by that?"

She's jumpy, McCoy. Keep your cool. He met her gaze. "I had a fabulous night with you, Heather, but I was referring to the kickboxing."

A deep pink stained her cheeks, but she maintained eye contact. "And I had a fabulous night with you, but it only happened because of the near-death experience."

Gotcha. "You mean having sex with any guy on the street would have been okay?"

Silence. He actually saw her think, watched her expressions change until only distaste remained.

"Well, no… of course not. But, we're not in love

or anything. I mean, I like you more than I used to, McCoy, and I have no regrets about last night, but don't start hearing wedding bells." She blushed again. "You are looking at a woman who will not date a cop, who will not live with a cop and who certainly will not fall in love with a cop. Get it?"

He leaned back in his chair, relaxed. "Too late, Heather. Last night, when I held you in my arms, you weren't thinking about McCoy, the cop. You were thinking about Dave, the man. And sweetheart, that's me, too." She stared as though he were speaking a foreign language.

"Eat your breakfast, McCoy. I've got a busy day ahead checking out the Girlfriends complex."

"I'm going, too."

She glared at him. "I don't need a watchdog."

He held up his hands in protest. "I know that. The new shelter is simply in my beat."

THAT AFTERNOON, Mary Beth leafed through the pages of her journal, studying the brief entries she'd made since arriving at Welcome Home five days earlier.

> Tuesday: Entered the shelter. Met Heather Marshall, my case worker. She's nice. Saw the doctor. The kids and I slept in our own apartment.

Wednesday: We're the ones living in a prison, when Hank is the one who should be put away. It's a nice enough place, but every window here is locked and the curtains are drawn. At least I'm walking better. Except for meals, Neil and Megan and I stayed together in our little apartment all day. The food was fine, and the kids ate. It's weird how we're surrounded by strangers, but the women look just like me. Worried, confused, shell-shocked.

Thursday: After breakfast, most of the other women went to various activities. I don't know what. The kids and I went outside to the back patio, which has tables and chairs. There's also a big yard and a vegetable garden. The kids played on the swings and slide, and I picked zucchini, yellow squash and tomatoes—enough to fill a grocer's bin. With some mushrooms and eggplant, I could make a nice ratatouille. Then the kids' tutor joined us. Young, pretty and full of smiles. The kids liked her. She brought some books and stayed awhile. They'll meet with her and the children every morning. Good.

Friday: I woke up crying. I dreamed about my friends and my parents. They must be worrying by now. I wonder what Hank has told them. But I'm glad I left. I can breathe here. And that's what I said in Group this morning. My first group session with other women who have recently come to the shelter.

I sat on a worn leather couch between two other women, and I listened as they told their stories. Theirs sounded like mine. They used the word *victim* over and over, and for the first time, I feel as if I'm one, too. I didn't cause this. I'm not too stupid to live. I'm not guilty. More important, I know these women will believe everything I tell them. I started to cry, and Heather passed me the tissues. There's a box of tissues in every room.

Saturday: The kids want to live here forever. Heather says we can stay as long as we need to. But Neil is still convinced his daddy will find us despite the walls, the cameras and the locks that make our prison safe. Hank did an excellent job brainwashing our son—in brainwashing all of us. That we couldn't have secrets from him. And if we lied, he'd find out sooner or later, and then we'd pay. We've already paid so much.

Sunday: I took the kids to the small chapel here this morning. It's really just a converted classroom. The service was nondenominational and perfect for this place. Most people showed up. No mystery about what everyone was praying for! Then I got a surprise. When the prayers were over, and the leader sat down, the singing started. Some ladies have very fine voices and no hesitation about using them. The room rocked with a gospel beat. When was the last time I enjoyed music?

Mary Beth closed her diary, satisfied she'd written exactly what had happened and how she'd felt each day of the first week. She would continue to write, to keep a record. And when this crazy period was over, she'd be able to look back and marvel that she and the kids had survived. It was a nice dream—a miracle really—and it would keep her going. But she couldn't allow herself to hope too hard. Not as long as Hank wore the uniform.

"I'VE GOT DRAW-DOWN MONEY for capital expenditures," said Heather, "but the place looks worse than I remember. At least on the outside."

She and Dave stood on the sidewalk looking at the brick-faced house which would become Girlfriends. The building had a wide wraparound porch and four apartments—two over two—each with three bedrooms. A center entrance revealed a front hall; a door on each side opened to an apartment. A staircase led to the second-floor units. The front and backyards had grown wild. Weeds were starting to consume the cement sidewalk, too.

"With Houston's eleven-month growing season, what did you expect?" Dave asked. "And don't wade through the lawn. It's ankle deep. Fire ants, rodents, snakes...no telling what's living there now."

"Happy thought. Now, remind me why I let you tag along."

"My charm?" He grinned, and she shook her in mock exasperation.

They each recognized the accord behind their banter. Despite her protests, she'd been afraid to be alone. Not that she would have admitted it, not at any cost. It was stupid. Really stupid. The perp was behind bars. But what if he had more friends? What if those friends knew where he'd been going? What if...

Dave had told her to write a novel. With her

imagination, she'd sell it to Hollywood and make a cool million.

So she'd gone with him back to his apartment. He lived a good twenty minutes southwest of her, off Westheimer, in a lovely complex of two-story buildings with a swimming pool and tennis courts.

His apartment was sparsely furnished, but there were pictures on the walls, and the place looked more like a home than a pit stop.

While he took a shower, Heather had looked around.

It seemed that Dave actually lived in his living room. Magazines covered the coffee table, the remote control for the television on top of them. The book shelves had just what she imagined a cop would read. Thrillers. Police procedurals. Mysteries. Horror. Great authors. Too good, in fact. They made their stories so real, she could only read them in small chunks.

She'd wandered to his movie collection. And that's when she was so surprised, she had to look twice. A collection of comedies—DVDs and cassettes—filled two shelves. Comedies of all kinds. Laugh-out-loud slapstick, smart romantic comedies.

Heather was too cynical to really believe in all these happily-ever-after endings, but at least they were hopeful stories.

Regardless of her personal beliefs, Dave was a Jekyll and Hyde character in his tastes. Interesting. He was a lot more complicated than she'd expected.

"You're going to need a load of tools to straighten this up," said Dave, kicking at a weed, "or else hire a lawn service."

"A volunteer army is what we're talking about." She took out her pad and a pen and wrote, Landscaping. "Let's start with the tools first." Mower, edger, trimmer, rakes, gloves, plastic bags.

"Don't forget about wearing closed shoes. Boots would be even better," said Dave. "Now, let's go inside."

Heather was eager to explore. She'd inspected each of the apartments when she wrote the grant, and knew the building had potential. A city engineer had accompanied her, talking about building codes, electricity, beams, windows. Her key turned in the lock, but Dave had to shoulder the door open.

Inside it was stuffy and warm, but the rooms in the first apartment were fairly clean. The four units were mirror images of each other, each with a large eat-in kitchen, dining room, living room and bathroom as well as three bedrooms.

"I want to break through some walls," said

Heather, leading Dave to the back of the apartment. "I want us all connected. Maybe the top floor can be set up with bedrooms for the kids, one for live-in staff and also a family room with a television. We can take out the kitchens up there and have more room for sleeping, socializing and studying."

"Then you want more than cosmetics, and you'll need a general contractor."

"And that'll cost me," Heather replied. "But it'll save money in the long run. If I operate four separate apartments, I'll need four employees. I can't leave the kids alone."

His eyebrow jerked upward, his eyes wide. "Teenage girls? Alone? A scary thought."

But she shook her head. "No, McCoy. They're not scary. They're just plain scared." She changed direction and ran her hand lightly along the wall as she led him back toward the entrance. "Once upon a time," she whispered, "I needed a place…"

"Tell me."

But she couldn't. The words choked her, and she looked at the floor. "It was a long time ago. It's all over now. And I'm here. I survived. Happy and healthy." She made an effort to lighten up. "My only trouble seems to be with weapon-toting drug runners."

"Hey, kiddo. That's my department."

"I'm glad you came back in time." Her voice dropped. "I'm sorry you got hurt. I could feel the impact of each strike from where I stood."

He shrugged. "Well, I'm a big boy. I can defend myself." He tapped her on the nose and grinned. "Or anyone that needs help."

"Yes, I know." She managed a smile. "You throw a good punch." If he ever got angry and needed a target… He was almost twice her size. He could knock her out with one heavy swing if she didn't see it coming.

"Heather…"

The concern in his voice got her attention. "What?" She still didn't look up.

"Please," he said softly. "Look at me. What are you thinking? What's wrong? Sure, I threw some punches, but I only did it in self-defense. And to protect you."

She said nothing.

"And you took some pretty hefty action yourself. And I thank you."

"Defense is justified," she mumbled. "Defense is the only reason…"

"I agree. So what's the problem?"

HEATHER COULDN'T SLEEP. She tossed on her bed, thinking about how happy Kathy and Mark had been when they'd returned from the Texas hill country earlier. Her sister had looked wonderful, sounded wonderful. Mark's parents had greeted her with affection, which was progress for his mother, who thought no woman worthy of her only son. When the couple had paused for breath, Heather reluctantly explained the damage to Kathy's car. Mark reacted first.

"The hell with the car." He took out his cell and started punching numbers. "First thing in the morning, Jim. A complete system—windows and doors. And I want the monitoring service to connect to the local HPD station house, not the big one downtown."

"That's what McCoy wanted us to do," whispered Heather to Kathy. "But it's Sunday night. How can Mark reach anyone?"

Kathy patted her hands. "There's a whole other world out there, Heather. I'm betting this Jim person provides security services for Mark's company—and that's a lot of buildings and other facilities."

"Kath," said Heather, as she first glanced at Mark, then tilted her head to stare at her sister, "you're going to be really rich."

Her sister shrugged. "I'm going to be really

happy." Kathy stared at her fiancé who was winding up the phone call. Her love for him was so visible that Heather blinked back tears.

Heather punched her pillow one more time. She doubted she would ever look at a man the way Kathy looked at Mark. She'd have to find her happiness in other areas—work, friends, the kids she helped, her family. She'd create her own definition of happiness.

So, what's the problem? Dave's question boomed in her head.

The problem was Heather and her judgment of men. She could spot the bozos in a heartbeat—and stood clear. But she rarely gave anyone else a chance; never if they wore a uniform. Until last night.

Last night, she'd slipped up. And today she discovered that McCoy liked to laugh. So now, she had to make sure nothing as sweet ever happened between them again.

CHAPTER SIX

DAILY ROUTINES brought an order to life. By the end of the following work week, Heather's confidence had rebounded, and she attacked each day with her usual energy. As she and Kathy left the house on Friday morning, she paused to set the new alarm system, then locked the door with her key from the outside—as they'd been taught. Mark had made them go through the steps three times, making them promise to set the alarm every time they left the house. They'd all memorized the code numbers.

"Notice my skill with that lock!" She grinned at her sister.

"The poor guy's been having nightmares," replied Kathy. "Don't be surprised if he wants to move in."

Heather laughed out loud. "Good excuse. Doesn't bother me at all."

Kathy's eyes twinkled, but she didn't say anything

until Heather had unlocked the car, and they were both inside.

"Speaking of moving," Kathy began, "...and don't answer right away...Mark and I would like you to consider moving in with us after the wedding." She rushed on. "The new house is certainly big enough, you'd have your own bedroom and bath—as much privacy as you'd want. And we wouldn't interfere with your social life...."

Heather stared at her sister in disbelief. "Are you nuts? We're lucky I haven't started the car 'cause I would have crashed into the mailbox." She turned the key in the ignition, and backed out of the driveway. "You two are really sweet, but I'm fine right here. I like this neighborhood."

"It's not the neighborhood we're worried about, Heather. It's you."

"But the men are all in jail or deported. I'll be safe, especially with the high-tech system we have."

"Until the next thing happens," grumbled Kathy.

"There won't be a next thing," said Heather as calmly as she could. "We're getting the new van in a few days, and I can spread the word about Girlfriends."

"You mean you and a *partner* can spread the word."

"Absolutely—and I'm not kidding. For all our sakes."

"Too bad Officer McCoy's on duty nights. I bet he'd volunteer to tag along with you every time."

As if she'd allow that. "No thanks. He'd scare the kids away."

"Not if he were out of uniform…and the boys might relate to him better. You never know."

Heather pulled into the driveway of Welcome Home. "He's only off duty on weekends, but it doesn't matter. Even I know when my plate's too full to pile on more. I can't go out on Saturday or Sunday now. There's so much work ahead of me at Girlfriends—my weekends won't be my own for months, if ever."

Kathy's wedding in December would wind up being a welcome distraction.

Heather got out of the car and looked at the building. Everything else could wait. "Right now," she said, "I've got a group of women who need one another."

MARY BETH CLUTCHED a ball of tissues in her sweaty hands as she entered the brightly lit meeting room. Her heart raced like a thoroughbred crossing the finish line, but she made herself smile at Kimberly and Tashika, who had arrived ahead of her. Both were about her age, and had already sat in their usual club chairs.

"Am I late?" Mary Beth asked, before noticing that Heather and Connie weren't there yet. She took her own place on the leather couch. A blue area rug covered most of the floor, and a wood coffee table held some magazines, paper, pencils and a box of tissues. In this room, too, the walls were decorated with large colorful prints.

Both women shook their heads, and murmured a hello. Mary Beth understood their reticence. Being part of this group was hard work. The women were probably gearing up for what lay ahead. Just as she was.

After three prior sessions, today she would speak up for the first time. So far, she'd offered only her name. Her first name. And that had been enough. A phony name would have been fine, too. But now she needed to do more.

The hard part was getting her story started, deciding how to relate her fifteen years with Hank so that the women would understand. They probably viewed cops as allies.

She glanced toward the doorway as Heather walked in, with her ready smile and a bucketful of energy. It was always that way with Heather

Marshall. But, well…she was so young. So pretty. And Mary Beth felt very old inside. She barely glanced in the mirror anymore for fear of seeing the old woman reflected there. She was thirty-seven.

"Hi, everyone." Heather pulled over a straight-back chair. "We're not waiting for Connie this morning, and I'll tell you why in a moment. But first, I want to know about breakfast. Did you eat it?"

Huh? What was this about?

"I did," said Heather. "It wasn't so great."

The other women smiled, but no one complained.

"Anyone want to work with the cook?" asked Heather, looking from one woman to the next. "We need someone with culinary talent. Stella needs serious help now that we've got so many residents here. I'm talking about menu decisions and actual main course preparation. Other people can set the tables, clean up and do the simpler food prep."

"Me." Shocked, Mary Beth realized it was her voice she heard, her arm in the air.

"Thank you, Mary Beth." Heather smiled at her. "I was hoping you'd volunteer. Two of our youngest residents told me you're the best cook in the world. After we finish here, I'll introduce you to Stella."

Tashika interrupted in her distinctive soft drawl.

"Now can you tell us where Connie is?" The woman collapsed back in her chair as if she could have taken a nap. But Tashika's brain kept on spinning no matter how relaxed her body looked.

"Connie had some good news this morning," said Heather.

Silence.

"Her abuser was arrested last night. No bail. Connie's with our legal team. She's considering testifying against him in court."

"Hot damn!" said Tashika. The other women grinned.

"Why was he arrested?" asked Mary Beth quietly. "Was it for something he'd done to Connie?"

Heather shook her head, her eyes shadowed. "He'd victimized someone else. Another woman. He was beating her up, and somebody called the police. When they got there, he fired his weapon, and they brought him down. The woman's in the hospital, and so is he...under guard."

"Connie's free," Mary Beth breathed. "She can take back her life. Her abuser will never see sunlight again. He shot at a cop, and he'll die in jail."

"Well, I don't know about that, but cops do take care of their own," said Kimberly.

"They sure do," said Mary Beth, grateful for the natural opening in the conversation. She stood up, walked behind the couch and grasped the frame. "I can tell you all you want to know about cops and why I couldn't go to the police department for help. Well, I did, once. But it didn't—work."

"Why not?" Tashika asked.

She gulped for breath. "They didn't exactly believe me. Let's say, they didn't *want* to believe me because my abuser…my husband…is a cop." All the air in her lungs was gone. Her fingers hurt from gripping the sofa. Mary Beth stared at the other two residents, and they stared back at her. Tears started to trickle down her cheeks.

"Oh, my goodness," said Kimberly. "I never thought about what that situation might be like."

"Then, I'll tell you," replied Mary Beth. "I need to tell you." She paused to gather her thoughts. "Hank had on-the-job training to keep people under control. And he used it at home. Not always with his hands. Sometimes his face changed, and he got that crazy look in his eyes, and he yelled…I was terrified. And I did what he wanted. At other times, he used his voice—different tones meant different things. One minute he was loving, and the next minute…he was like a chameleon changing himself whenever he wanted to. I never knew what to expect. He once handcuffed me to the leg of the bedroom armoire and left the house. I lay on the floor, I couldn't move the dresser. And my kids...my kids were due home from school...."

God, she hadn't thought about that for a long time. How Neil kept calling her and finally he and Megan came into her bedroom and she'd made a game of playing with them on the floor. Reading to them, drawing with them. Until Daddy got home an hour later and told the kids that their mom did such a great job cleaning, that she threw out the key to his big bracelet. And he'd had to go to the store and get another one.

She'd hated him then. She hated him now.

"You know what he said when I threatened to call the police?" No one said a word. "He laughed at me. Laughed at me." She grabbed the sofa again. "He dared me to call the station house. 'Who do you think they'll believe?'" he said. "'I've already told my buddies that you're depressed and acting loony.'"

Her tissues were shredded, but she wiped her cheeks. "And he was right," she whispered. "I went down there, and no one believed me." She choked back a sob. "No one will ever believe me."

"I believe you," said Tashika.

"So do I," Kimberley added.

Mary Beth nodded, words too much for her at the moment. Then she glanced at Heather. The young woman looked pale. Almost ill. Oh, God, no! "Ms. Heather, are you changing your mind? Can I still stay here?"

THE TERROR in Mary Beth's voice instantly brought Heather back from Dry Creek. And the memory of her intoxicated father backhanding her against the wall, shoving her in her bedroom and locking his cuffs on her wrists so she couldn't leave through the window.

"Of course, you can stay, Mary Beth," said Heather. "Absolutely. And I'm so sorry I scared you. Your story reminded me…of someone…who used to be in law enforcement."

Mary Beth almost fell into her seat.

She'd upset the group. Angry with herself, Heather thought of a dozen ways she could have responded to the distraught woman. She was supposed to facilitate the discussion, not become part of the discussion. But the women were waiting for some kind of response, and she couldn't leave them in limbo, ignoring their feelings.

"This man—this lawman—lived in the small town where I grew up, and he acted exactly the way Mary Beth described her husband acting. So, yes, Mary Beth, I believe everything you've said."

The woman smiled and settled back on the couch, her body relaxed. Heather reminded herself how fragile her clients were, how long they had to climb toward self-confidence.

"Cops are cops," said Tashika. "Small towns, big cities. Don't matter. They're the boss."

"What about the law?" asked Heather, back in her role as facilitator. "Isn't the law supposed to be the boss?"

And that got the discussion going about their personal experiences and where they legally stood now in relation to their abusers.

Kimberley finally pointed at Mary Beth. "You need to get a restraining order. You need to get a divorce."

"I went for help once—to the station house—after he hit me, and the officers called it a little family problem. The captain wasn't there at the time, but I never went back. It seems to me that when a regular person beats up his wife, it's a crime. When a cop beats up his wife, it's a 'family problem.' Double standards."

Mary Beth was coming alive. Anger and indignation filled her voice. Excellent signs. She was fighting for her self-esteem, fighting for her rights as a human being.

She'd taken a big step that day, and Heather's job was to lead her the rest of the way. Help her find a happy ending for her and the children even if it meant relocation. Mary Beth was safe now, and their legal team would help her file a restraining order. But under no circumstances could Officer Hank Landers ever discover that his wife and children lived at Welcome Home. Which meant that she could never admit it to Officer Dave McCoy regardless of his suspicions.

"DAVID! Are you in love with her?"

Dave stared at his mom across the table, glad he hadn't started to drink his piping-hot coffee. They were at The Mason Jar, a favorite low-key lunch place that was also convenient to the construction company where Anne managed the office. "In love with her?" he repeated. "I never said that."

He waited while Anne folded her napkin and placed it beside her plate. Her gray eyes studied him. "You've mentioned Heather's name at least a dozen times since we've sat down." She tapped her watch. "Twenty-five minutes. I'd say that means something." Then she bestowed a brilliant smile on him, a smile that could still turn heads. "You're my son. I love you with all my heart. I also know you."

"Oh." *Eloquent, McCoy.* "Well, maybe I mentioned her a lot because she's driving me crazy. Always getting into trouble, but, somehow it's not usually her fault. She's like a—a one person patrol district all by herself. I need to clone myself to keep up with her. But at least she's got that alarm system in now."

His gentle mother clasped his hands and held on tightly. "David, my wonderful David. More than anything in the world, I want you to be happy. So, tell me, how does Heather feel about you?"

He didn't know, and he didn't know how to respond. "I'm…I'm working on it."

Anne's eyes clouded, and Dave had a hard time getting the next sentence out. "She hates my job."

"Then quit."

Startled, Dave sat back and stared at her. The gracious and serene woman who had become as much his friend as his parent wasn't serene right now.

"Just like that? Leave the department?" He must have misunderstood. The department was his career, and she knew it.

But Anne's head bobbed assent as she waved to the server. "Check, please. Don't argue," she said to Dave. "I'm getting this one. Let's take a walk."

He placed his palm against her cheek. "Mom. Calm down. You haven't even finished eating. We can talk later."

She stood up, brushing his hand aside. "We're leaving. I can't eat, and I can't calm down until you listen to me."

Five minutes later, they rounded a corner away from the busy street. His mom was setting the pace, her long legs eating up the sidewalk. Dave walked easily beside her.

"Your father..." she began, and Dave groaned. "Your father has become a better man since he retired two years ago. Are you aware, David, that he barely talks about his career anymore? Barely mentions the job or the friends he's made from the time he started on the street. It's like the whole thirty years never happened."

Dave saw a flash of pain cross her face, but she kept walking.

"Once upon a time," Anne continued, "the job was the only topic in our house. It was his world, and he loved everything about it. He never noticed the stress. But dead bodies take a toll. And what happened to him also happened to me.

"But now, he's different. Have you noticed he hardly takes a drink anymore? And he doesn't yell anymore. He laughs a lot instead. He's almost the same man he was before you were born." Her voice faded, her eyes seemed unfocused and dreamy.

Dave watched her and listened, astounded. She sounded happy, and looked so animated while she told him about Patrick running track and swimming laps.

"I think he's decompressing from thirty years on the force," said Anne, halting her speed-walk. She poked Dave in the chest with her finger. "Dad hasn't even gone after another job! Not security, not a small-town sheriff's position, not even a part-time gig. He's had enough." His mom finally stepped back, and took a breath, a deep breath, which she obviously needed after her nonstop recital.

He loved his mother, but her story was only half-right. His dad was drinking a lot less—that was true. When Patrick and Dave got together, however, their conversations centered mainly on the department, and that's where his mom was wrong. His dad was up-to-date on everything Dave was doing, had encouraged him to take the sergeant's exam. Patrick was in touch with all his old buddies, everyone he'd ever worked with who was still in Houston. And some who'd moved away.

"He does seem more relaxed," said Dave, "since he retired. I agree with you about that." He wasn't going to enlighten his mom about where Patrick's interests really lay. "So, how do you know all this? About his so-called change of habits. About his swimming laps and going to the gym? You've been divorced for a million years."

She glanced briefly at him and began walking again at a much slower pace. "Does it seem like a million years to you? Well, it must. You were what? Twelve years old?"

Dave nodded but bit his tongue.

"Your dad and I have never been enemies, David. I got out when I saw what his career was doing to him. To us. To the family. In those days, you dreaded him coming through the door at the end of his shift." She stopped and bent to adjust her shoe before looking at him. "Is that what you want with your Heather? A great relationship and a great family that goes to hell because of a stupid job? Leave the force, David. You don't have to follow in your dad's footsteps. He won't be disappointed. If that's what concerns you, I promise you it won't matter to him."

His mom was a locomotive at times, racing down the track to her destination without blowing her whistle. He needed to catch up.

He addressed her last remark first. "I never thought of leaving the job, so disappointing him is not an issue."

Anne patted his arm. "Well, in case you're considering it, now you won't have to be concerned."

"Mom...you haven't answered my question. How do you know all these details of his retired life? Have you guys been talking?"

His mother blushed like a young girl. Looked like a young girl, too, at that moment. Man, he'd just uncovered dynamite—and he sure didn't want to hold a lit match to it.

"He joined my health club," Anne replied. "We swim together."

"I see..." He wasn't going down that road. "Say, I didn't realize the time. How about I drive you back to work?"

"Sure," said Anne. "I like a captive audience. Take the long way to the office."

RETIRED POLICE Lieutenant Patrick McCoy strapped his revolver around his ankle, pocketed his wallet and glanced in the mirror. More gray strands seemed to sprout up every week, but Anne thought he looked distinguished. The word made him grin. And thinking about Annie made his grin jack-o-lantern wide. Either he was one lucky son of a gun, or he was one smooth operator. He shook his head. Smooth operator? If he were so smooth, he never would have lost her in the first place. *Learn from the past, old fool, but live in the present.* Sometimes, retirement meant new beginnings. His life was looking up.

He checked the clock radio on his night table. Too early, again. He had to laugh at himself. Every time he had a date with Anne, he felt like an anxious teenager out to impress the homecoming queen. The comparison wasn't far off. He'd dated plenty of women in the past fifteen years—some very nice women—but no one came close to taking Anne's place. His ex-wife would always be the one in his heart, and this time around, he wouldn't screw it up. This time, Annie would come first. When she'd called earlier to ask if he were free, he bowed out of his weekly poker game with the boys.

He grabbed his key ring, and a few minutes later left

his subdivision and drove the several miles to the town house development where Anne lived. After their son had moved out, Anne hadn't wanted the responsibility of home ownership. Mowing a lawn every week was not for her. So, five years ago, she'd sold the house she and Patrick had bought when David was a little boy.

Of course, Anne had every right to sell it. But when Patrick had seen the rooms taken apart with boxes everywhere, it had torn his heart. He'd never said a word, but Annie knew. She'd looked right through him and said, "Buck up, Lieutenant. You're a decade too late."

His Annie had become a strong woman since the divorce. Heck, Anne had always had enough self-confidence to refuse accepting second place. She'd washed her hands of him, but for David's sake, had remained friends. It seemed, however, that marriage was something she didn't want to try again. Maybe he'd given her a bad taste for the male species, or maybe, just maybe, she still had a soft spot for him. He was doing his best to find out.

He pushed the button next to the security gate connected to Anne's apartment, noting how all the names and buttons were displayed in the open. Such a poor design from a safety standard. There should be an entry code that a visitor had to know. And the gate itself stayed open as long as cars rolled in, so a bunch of unidentified vehicles could easily follow Patrick. Of course, they wouldn't, because Patrick would get out of the car and chat with anyone behind him.

Anne's voice came through the speaker startling him. "Patrick? Is that you?"

She'd never learn. She trusted the whole damn world. He bit his tongue, did not say it was Jack the Ripper at the door. "Yes, Annie. It's me."

"Come on up." She buzzed him in and was waiting in her doorway when he arrived, smiling, her hair full of reflected light, her gray eyes smoky.

And he lost his breath, as usual. She never failed to capture his attention in every way.

"Hi." His voice sounded husky.

"Come in," she invited, leading the way. "I thought we could have dinner here tonight, outside on the patio. The weather's perfect."

And then he noticed her apron and the delicious aroma in the air. "Sold."

"It's not gourmet," she said with laughter in her voice, "but you're basically a meat-and-potato man, and I know you always liked my special meatloaf."

Oh, yeah. "And twice baked…?"

She nodded before he could finish the question. He suddenly wondered if she was setting him up. But for what?

"Some wine?" she offered, reaching into the fridge.

"I'll wait for dinner. So, were you just in the mood to play in the kitchen today?"

She handed him two large plates with cutlery and nodded toward the patio. "Not especially. I wanted to speak privately with you."

He'd known she had to have a reason for a private tête-à-tête, but he was disappointed. When he came back inside, he asked, "What did you want to talk about?"

"David."

Her serious tone scared him. "Is something wrong? I had lunch with him two days ago, and he looked great."

"He's fine, Patrick. Healthy. Really. But…he's in love."

"He's what?" His voice reflected his shock. How could he have missed that little factor in his son's life?

Anne started to giggle. "Oh, I'm so glad I wasn't the last one to figure it out. In fact, David may be the last to know."

His brain hurt. Dave had a girlfriend and didn't

know it? But as he watched Anne's expressive face light up, he almost forgot he had a son. It was the mother who held him captive.

"You're the most beautiful woman I know," he said, startling himself.

Startling her. She waved the compliment away. "I want to talk about David."

He nodded and waited until the food and wine were transferred to the outdoor table. "So, what do you think I know that you don't?" he asked.

"Who's Heather Marshall?"

"Heather Marshall!" He put his wineglass down with a clunk. "She's the one? Are you sure?"

"Yes."

Patrick stared at her serious face and started to laugh. He laughed so hard, he had to hold his stomach. "You've got to be kidding," he finally gulped. "It can't be her. She's the one driving him crazy. The one he's always looking out for, the one who was almost killed a time or two."

Her eyes widened at that. "She's done all that…and he still remains right there with her…like glue. And you say I've got to be kidding? Think!" Her satisfied smile told the story.

"You mean…?"

Anne nodded.

So, in the end, with all his deductive reasoning skills, he was a dumb male creature who knew squat about women.

"I told David to quit his job."

Words eluded him. Fifteen years disappeared. He and Annie were back where they'd left off.

CHAPTER SEVEN

HEATHER WASN'T SURE of the exact number of volunteers to expect on Saturday, but she packed her car with juice, water and boxes of doughnuts in case. A load of gardening tools and gloves filled her trunk. Gene was using their pickup truck to bring two lawn mowers—one new and one from the shelter.

As she drove to Girlfriends early in the morning, she reviewed all the folks she'd notified. She'd contacted every friend she had in Houston, from Sara Patterson to colleagues at other social service agencies. She'd brought posters to neighborhood churches announcing the need for help every weekend. The board of directors of Welcome Home were also pitching in to spread the word. And then there was Dave McCoy, who'd called her at the shelter the day before to remind her that he'd have a bunch of friends coming. She sighed. Just what she didn't need. Police officers scaring everyone else away.

No. Erase that thought. She needed to be fair. Dave's friends were hard workers; they knew what she was trying to do and they'd been supportive of the project. *So, don't mess up your volunteers, Heather.* She'd also asked Mark to research some contractors, and he'd promised to be in touch quickly. Today was the first Saturday of October, and she only had three months to get ready. Her target was New Year's Day. A new life for the kids.

"I don't think I've forgotten anything," she murmured to herself as she pulled up to the building. At seven-thirty, hers was the first car there. She got out and slowly looked around her. It was a quiet residential neighborhood. The homes across the street showed no outward signs of life yet. She checked for the house keys in her pocket, and in ankle-high boots toured the outside of the building. The grass had grown taller since last Sunday. As she stood on the sidewalk surveying the intimidating grounds, Heather realized for the very first time that she'd never owned a home before and hadn't the slightest idea how to garden.

She started to chuckle, then laughed out loud. She laughed at herself—at the absurdity of her ignorance. And maybe she laughed because the stress of the past week needed an escape valve. Tears dripped from her eyes and she wiped them with the back of her hands. Jumping into the deep end was so typical of her. Jumping in and believing that somehow the job would get done. "Oh, my, my, my."

"You sure got up on the right side of the bed today." A familiar masculine voice. "What's got you going so hard that you didn't even notice my truck?"

She turned in time to see McCoy's gorgeous grin. Gorgeous? When had anything about him become gorgeous to her?

"The bed's got nothing to do with it," she replied. "I'm an idiot."

"Hey, watch it! You're talking about my good friend, the intrepid Heather Marshall."

Intrepid. Heather shook her head and sighed. "I guess that's me, all right. More guts than brains sometimes." She led him to her car and reached for the refreshments. "Have a doughnut."

His eyes narrowed as he stared at her. "No cop jokes, please, and especially not from you."

"Huh?" She glanced at him, then at the box of sweets. "For crying out loud, I never thought of that."

"In that case…" He reached for one.

"So," began Heather conversationally, "is there any chance you know how to use a lawn mower?"

"A lawn mower? Of course I know how to run a lawn mower. *Everyone* knows how to run a lawn mower."

Not everyone, but she didn't have to enlighten him. "Well, McCoy. This morning, you're the go-to guy for lawns."

Another car pulled up. Then another. Within ten minutes, Heather had a dozen people around her. Three passed along Sara's regards. One was from the dealership supplying the new van. And several teenagers showed up from the local churches. Boys and girls. Then two police officers and their spouses—Heather had met them at Yorkie's house. Everyone was in high spirits, studying the challenge at their feet.

"We've got two mowers, so let's divide into two teams," said one man. He had a deep, confident voice. "And the clippings will need to be raked."

Heather glanced toward the speaker, a tall man with salt-and-pepper hair, and dark eyes that seemed to miss nothing. He nodded to her.

"Ms. Marshall, do we have any rakes?"

She nodded. "Yes."

"Right here," answered Gene at the same time. He started to distribute them.

"How about electricity?" asked the man. "Any outside sources to plug in the trimmers?"

"The electricity is on in the house," said Heather, "but I don't really know about outside connections. I'm sorry."

The man's smile seemed familiar. "Don't worry. We'll figure it out." He whipped out a pair of dark glasses and turned toward the gathering. As though waiting for a signal, two groups of volunteers emerged. Dave and the other man went to opposite sides of the building, each one pushing a mower. A half-dozen people, tools in hand, followed each man.

Heather looked at Gene. "Maybe they don't need us."

"Are you kidding? Give me the keys. I want to get a look inside one of these units."

"Thanks, Gene. I really appreciate the backup. And your time."

The older man actually blushed. "Just trying to keep you out of trouble," he grumbled.

"I swear I don't go looking for it." She laughed as she handed him the keys. Then she started hauling cleaning items out of her car.

Just as she slammed her trunk closed, she heard a noise like a gunshot and dropped to the ground. Her heart pounding, she peeked across the street, where a car backfired—again. Heather stood and brushed off her jeans, disgusted with herself.

KATHY APPEARED an hour later, a tentative smile pasted on her face. Heather braced herself. She wrung out the ammonia-soaked rag she was using to wash windows in one of the apartments and placed it over the pail.

"What's up?" she asked, peeling off her rubber gloves.

Kathy's smile brightened. "Well, I've got good news…and I've got bad news." Her smile faded.

"Let's go with the good news first," Heather said.

"You got a call from the Ford dealership. The new van is ready to be picked up. And it's paid for in full."

Now *that* was great news. "In full? Are you sure? I knew we had a big down payment, but…?"

Kathy nodded vigorously. "I'm absolutely certain. You had another donor. An anonymous donor." Her cheeks grew pink, and Heather chuckled.

"Anonymous, my foot. Mark, huh? He really shouldn't have. He's done enough for us already."

"He says it's an investment."

"In your mental health, I bet."

Kathy grinned and nodded. "There's that, but also an investment in the community. He can't give time, so he's giving what he can."

"Okay, okay. But I'm glad he'll at least get a tax deduction from it," replied Heather.

Kathy rolled her eyes.

"Kathy…I'm sorry. It's just hard for me right now." Heather started to pace. "I'm having a difficult time separating what people are doing for the new shelter from what people are doing for me, personally. I don't want to generate gifts for the wrong reasons. Especially from your new family."

Kathy paled. "You're still my family. I'm not leaving you…."

Heather reached for her hand and squeezed it hard. "I'm sorry. I didn't mean that the way it sounded. But maybe you're losing confidence in me after…everything. Maybe you think I'm the wrong person to head up Girlfriends now. The truth is I'm not even sure."

"Come with me into the sunshine for a moment," said Kathy. They walked to the doorway. "Now stay right here. I'll be back in half a minute."

And she was. With McCoy in tow. And another man. The other team leader.

"Would you tell Officer McCoy what you just said to me?" asked Kathy.

But her sister's words flew over her head. "Holy Toledo. There are two of you?"

Dave nodded. "This is my dad, Patrick. He knows construction and wants to help."

Heather nodded at the older man. "Thanks, but you look like a cop, not a construction worker."

"You've got a keen eye, Ms. Marshall. I'm retired HPD."

She looked from father to son. Dave would still be a handsome man in thirty years.

"What's wrong, Heather?" asked Dave. "What's Kathy talking about?"

She felt her face get warm. "It's nothing. Just that..." And then she told them all about the car backfiring, about looking over her shoulder since last Sunday. "And you know how I am about locking the doors now. And how stupid is that since the perps are in jail?"

The men didn't laugh. "PTSD," said Dave's dad.

"I think so," replied Dave. "At least a mild case."

He studied her. "Ever hear of post-traumatic stress disorder? It's what a lot of soldiers have after they've been in combat."

"Yes. Sure. I've got clients with the aftereffects of trauma. They're easily startled and it takes them a while to…let it go."

"Your clients have an advantage," said Dave. "They've got time to regroup, catch their breath. They're living in a safe house with a ten-foot wall. But you're back to work without a pause. Pretending everything is just like usual."

"But it's my job," protested Heather immediately. "It's what I do. I can't let the kids down."

A quiet moment passed until Patrick broke the stillness. "Son," he said, "this one's a keeper."

Dave's face reddened. "Next week you're staying home."

"Oh, no," replied Patrick. "I'm having too much fun. Besides, this place needs a lot of work. And as for you, Ms. Marshall, you may not live in a safe house, but as long as I'm around, your back is covered."

She wanted to believe him. She believed that *he* meant it. And he *seemed* like an okay guy. But she'd spent too many years distrusting the uniform. She wouldn't be awed by him. Or in debt to him. Or trust blindly because he was Dave's father. Particularly when she was almost certain he was carrying a weapon—just like his son.

"Thanks for your offer, Mr. McCoy," she said, meeting his gaze. "But will you answer a question for me?"

"If I can."

"Are you an honorable man?"

ANNE MCCOY'S TEMPER flared. Did she hear correctly—did that woman just ask her ex-husband if he was honorable? Her lips tightened. What kind of question…who would ask…? Was this the girl David had spoken about nonstop? She hoped not. This girl was rude and obviously had no instincts for people if she could think Patrick was dishonorable.

She held her anger and stood quietly in the silence that followed the question, watching the four in front of her at the entry to the building. She'd obviously arrived just in time. David and the dark-haired woman finally began to protest in unison. "Heather, how could you? Heather, you can't ask…" Anne's suspicions were confirmed. The blonde was the one.

"How can you ask such a question?" The brunette sounded embarrassed and glanced apologetically at Patrick. Anne wanted to hug her.

"I'm not taking any chances," Heather said.

"Then I would hope," said Dave in a strained tone,

"that you have the judgment to recognize the good in people." His eyes pierced her.

Anne cheered silently while she watched Heather tilt her head back to meet her son's challenge. The girl's expression softened a bit. Was there an apology being offered?

"I don't know him."

"But I do." Anne interrupted loudly enough so that all eyes turned toward her. "Patrick wore a shiny, untarnished badge for thirty years, and I'd trust him with my life—or yours. Honor has *never* been a problem with the men in my family—either of them." She walked forward, hand extended. "I'm Anne McCoy. I brought lunch."

DAVE'S MOM WAS TALL, slender and had gray eyes that resembled molten steel right now as she shook Heather's hand with a firm grip.

"They say timing is everything, Mrs. McCoy." Heather smiled. "It's nice to know you aren't afraid to protect your own. If there were more like you, I'd be out of business, and that would be great.... Thanks for the lunch. A very big thanks. I forgot all about it."

"I'm sure you had other details on your mind," replied Anne.

Kathy answered. "A million details, but that doesn't excuse how she attacked Lieutenant McCoy. I'm sorry about that." She shook Anne's hand. "I'm Kathy Marshall. Thanks for helping us."

Heather watched the instant rapport spring up between the two. She'd screwed up again.

"I want to talk to you," Dave said to her, "and we need privacy."

Uh-oh. She didn't like this. They walked a short distance from the others.

"What the hell were you doing back there?" Dave began. "My dad was offering to look out for you, and you spit in his face."

"I didn't…"

He glared at her.

"I didn't ask for a bodyguard," she said. "And I don't want one."

"He had the best of intentions, and you insulted him."

"Okay, I'll apologize—"

"Don't bother unless you're sincere. And then," he said, "you can figure out why you were so damn arrogant in the first place."

"I have a problem with cops."

"But we get along just fine," he replied.

"Since when?"

At his knowing expression, she felt heat rise to her face. They were becoming friends, and she was scared. Maybe she'd used Patrick to push him away. On and off duty, Dave was complicating her life. But his dad did deserve her apology.

They returned to the group in time to hear Anne say, "Looks like we've got our work cut out for us."

"We?" asked Patrick.

"And why not?" Anne said. "Why should you and David have all the fun turning this house into a home?"

And that's when unexpected tears rolled down Heather's face. "You understand," she whispered. "A home. Not an institution." She quickly wiped her cheeks. She looked at Anne, then Patrick. "Thank you both for that."

"No thanks needed," said Patrick. "Children need a real home."

"Well, just look at that," said Kathy. "Tears. You've made quite an impression on my little sister, Mrs. McCoy."

"I've got something in my eye," protested Heather. "Come on. Let's get everyone together for lunch. And then I'll tell them…no, wait a minute…." Heather looked at Anne. "You said it in just the right way. How about I'll introduce you, and you give a pep talk to the volunteers. I'm hoping they'll come back next Saturday."

Anne tilted her head. "Are you sure? I don't know much about it…."

"You're the original genuine homemaker," said Patrick. "You're perfect." Admiration laced his tone, his expression. Patrick McCoy was beaming at his ex for anyone to see, as though he were as deeply in love with her as he must have been thirty years ago.

"I'm not perfect, as you well know," corrected Anne, her eyes sparkling. "But I can probably rally the troops."

Heather glanced at Dave who looked stunned. His head moved from one parent to the other and back again as though he were at Wimbledon.

"What's…what's going on here?" he asked.

"Lunch!" responded Heather, taking his hand. "Let's go get the food." She pulled him with her, Kathy joining them.

"Are you sure they're divorced?" she joked when they were out of earshot.

"Whew!" said Kathy. "I could feel the heat, and I don't even know them."

"What the hell was that all about?" Dave opened

his mother's car and released the trunk lock. He walked to the back and peered inside. "Good Lord. She's brought enough food for a month."

"Food is how she thinks she can help," said Kathy. "You don't have to be a genius to see that she wants to jump into this project with you and your dad, Officer McCoy."

"Call me Dave."

"Okay, Dave."

But Dave seemed to be somewhere else. He looked back at his folks. "They're sleeping together."

"Which isn't against the law," said Heather with a grin.

But Dave wasn't smiling. Instead, he seemed disturbed. "They pulled me apart when I was a kid. The arguing never let up. Dad giving orders, and Mom telling him to shove it. Then I bounced from one house to the other, always worrying about the one who was alone...and now they blithely fall into bed with each other as though nothing had ever happened? What kind of a joke is that?"

Heather reached for his arm and squeezed gently. "Divorce is never a joke to anyone involved. Not to the parents, and especially not to the children. I'm sure it wasn't an easy decision for them."

She felt his muscles lock, thought he was going to pull away. But his other arm came up around her, as tense as the first.

"Look how they're walking next to each other," he said. "So naturally, so in step. If it weren't for having a kid, they'd never have split up."

"So now you think it's your fault?" She placed her palm gently against his cheek. "Look at me, Dave. Children always think family problems are their fault, but they never are. Adults are the ones with the power to make decisions."

"Try telling that to a twelve-year-old who loves them both."

"But you're not twelve years old anymore," Kathy said.

"True." He glanced toward his parents again. "It's weird how the past can catch up and surprise us. Like a familiar jacket that doesn't fit anymore."

"You're right," said Kathy. "An unwelcome memory." She reached for a box of sandwiches, then glanced at Heather, a worried expression on her face. "Remember that other news I had to tell you? The bad news?"

Heather's stomach rolled. "Oh, God. What? Has George bought the house next door to us?"

Kathy's startled expression was enough of a clue. Heather almost didn't need the details. "Not quite. He and Mama are coming to visit. Next weekend."

Heather's hands continued to unload packages from Anne's car, but she moved like a robot.

"Heather? Honey? Did you hear me?" Kathy's voice seemed to come from far away.

"I wasn't expecting them before the wedding," Heather finally said. "I would have been prepared by then." Her brain began to shift into gear. "Okay, Kathy. Not a problem. They'll take my room. I'll stay at Welcome Home." She slammed the trunk shut. "And God help you when you introduce them to Mark's parents."

"They have no power over Mark and me," replied Kathy. "But they sure seem to have power over you. Is ten years not long enough? Can't you move on?"

CHAPTER EIGHT

HEATHER GLANCED at the calendar in her office. Thursday. She and Kathy had barely spoken since Saturday, and the silence haunted her.

The intercom on her desk buzzed, interrupting her thoughts. Lisa Connors was in the reception area, right on time for her three o'clock appointment. Earlier that week, she'd been somewhat surprised to hear from her, but more surprised by Lisa's news that Eve was pregnant. She and Larry were thrilled, and the good news was the tipping point for Lisa's decision. She'd be relocating to Houston and wanted to chat about possible jobs.

She greeted Eve Hannity's sister with warmth and curiosity. "Will your sister be leaving the force?" asked Heather after they were back in her office.

"Are you kidding?" replied Lisa. "Eve loves her job and, from what I hear, she's top-notch."

Heather nodded, but didn't comment.

"So a temporary leave of absence is more like it. My sister's got the energy of a tornado. One little baby won't hold her back."

"Babies require a lot of work, though," said Heather. "They can exhaust you."

"Don't I know it. At Children's Protective Services, it's hard to overlook." She leaned forward confidentially. "I think this baby can use an auntie nearby. Eve's my only sister—my only sibling. And Larry's family lives in Colorado."

And Kathy was Heather's only sibling. She and Mark would probably have children one day, too. But Heather wouldn't be needed as much. Not with Mark's large family in Houston. A profound sense of loss filled her. Regret. If she and Kathy continued not to speak, how would she grow close to nieces and nephews? The current situation had to be rectified.

"Would you excuse me for a moment, Lisa?"

Heather stepped across the hall. Kathy looked up from her desk. "Could we meet later, just to talk?" asked Heather. She checked her watch. "How about over supper about six?"

But Kathy shook her head. "I have an errand. Eight o'clock at the house would be better."

Heather nodded. "See you later." She returned to her office and to Lisa Connors.

"So, tell me about your background and what you're looking for." Heather sat back to listen and ask questions. And then she said, "Let me tell you about Girlfriends." By the time she finished, she had another volunteer to ride in the brand-new van with her the following Monday. If references checked out, she possibly had her first hire for the teen shelter. A satisfying afternoon.

Heather ended her day when hunger pangs drove her from the office. She left the building, and there was McCoy, waving a bag from Jason's Deli at her. She covered ground in double time.

"How do you manage to know my schedule every day?" she asked, reaching for half a pastrami sandwich. "Mmm. Delicious."

He chuckled. "You're too easy, kiddo."

Heather leaned against his car, sandwich in one hand, soda in the other. "So tell me the secret. How do you know when I'm leaving when I don't even know until the last minute sometimes?"

"I've got clout. Plus insider info."

Her eyes widened. "Who's the mole?"

"The mole?" He cracked up. "Just a simple informer…and I can't tell. Might put me in danger," he whispered.

She grinned. Recently, having an escort wasn't a bad idea. "I never thought I'd say it, or rather, need to say it, but thanks. I'm much better, though. No more panicking. I went to a two-hour kickboxing class Monday night. Sweated my butt off, but the class worked wonders. Helped get my confidence back."

"But—"

She held up her hand. "I know. I know. Guns. Knives. I understand. I can use my head, too."

His eyes lit with…pride? And his voice was husky when he said, "If I weren't on duty, I'd kiss you…and hold you…. You're like no other woman I've known."

He couldn't be lying, not with the life she'd led. "A lot weirder than all the others, huh?"

His smile grew, jacking up her heart rate. "Not weirder. Just…more interesting. And a lot cuter." He tapped her nose.

She didn't have a lot of practice in flirting. Was he simply flirting? He seemed so sincere. *When in doubt, shut up.* Heather opted to finish her meal in silence.

"It's almost dark," said Dave. "Come on. I'll follow you home."

"I'm okay. You don't have to—"

"I want to. You're in my territory. And so far, it's been a quiet night."

She glanced toward the front seat of the patrol car. The radio had been on constantly, emitting information that didn't seem to concern McCoy. She shrugged. "Okay, I'll get my car."

"Just a sec. I almost forgot to tell you..." The timbre of his voice had changed. He was back in cop mode and examining her closely.

"What?"

"There's been buzz all over the department—and Heather, I mean throughout the city—about this cop's wife and kids who went missing. The guy's frantic."

Two could play this game. She adopted a blank stare, looked him straight in the eye while she lied without remorse. "His problems have nothing to do with me or Welcome Home."

He studied her, his expression calculating. "I mentioned this case once before and have my own opinion."

She began to protest, but he waved her to be quiet. "If—and I say if—she does show up with the children, you might need help."

"I'll keep that in mind." If Dave thought she'd trust the boys in blue with the fragile lives of three injured people, he needed to think again. But she chose to be polite and not insult the department. “Thanks again for the dinner. It hit the spot.” She began walking toward her car.

“Hang on,” he called after her. When she turned, he handed her his business card. “You can call the station house directly, and my cell number is on the back.” And then, as if he couldn’t resist, he brushed her cheek very gently. “Take care of yourself.”

She saw him in her rearview mirror until she pulled into her driveway behind Kathy’s car. He waited for her to get out and open her front door. After she’d waved at him, he finally took off. She wasn’t used to anyone looking after her. It felt strange…a nice kind of strange.

HEATHER CLOSED THE DOOR behind her and took a few steps down the center hall toward the kitchen. “Kathy,” she called. “I’m home.” And that’s when she heard several voices. She recognized Kathy, but she couldn’t quite place the other two. She took another step. And then Kathy was there, excited, and reaching for her hand.

“Come on in, Heather. Look who’s here a day early.”

Heather paused in the kitchen entry and looked at the startling tableau. At the table, drinking coffee and eating apple pie, sat George and Jolene, laughing and acting as though they didn't have a trouble in the world. As though they belonged in her home. Their faces were thinner, but they looked healthy enough. George still had thick sandy hair, but alcohol had left reddish-purple veins around his nose. They both looked up at her, eager.

"Well, well," said Heather, staying where she was. "Just look what the west wind blew into town." She shifted her stance and stared at her sister, wondering how Kathy could pull such a fast one on her. "A little warning would have been appreciated."

Kathy flinched. "It was important that we all get together before the wedding." She shrugged. "They just came earlier than planned."

"Enjoy yourselves."

Heather walked to her bedroom and locked the door behind her. How often had she wished for strong locks when she was a child? She packed her overnight bag and retraced her steps.

Her mother stood in the hallway now, her blue eyes clear but as faded as the checked blouse she wore. Her skin was sun darkened, the crow's feet around her eyes well defined. She rubbed her hands with quick movements. "Heather... Heather. Please. Let me look at you. You're so beautiful. Oh, it's been a long time." She raised her arms toward her daughter.

Heather stepped around her. "Kathy will get you some clean linen. You'll be comfortable—and *safe*—in there." She nodded at the bedroom.

Jolene looked stricken, and she let her arms fall to her sides. "But Heather, he's not like that anymore. We don't drink anymore. We're in recovery."

Heather paused and looked back at her mother. "Good for you, Jolene. Did you finally decide that black-and-blue wasn't such a pretty color after all?"

The sound of the woman's sobs followed Heather out the door. Once at her car, she threw her bag in the backseat.

"Proud of yourself?" Kathy had come after her, her voice full of accusation. "She has about as many defenses as a newborn baby."

"Proud of yourself, Kathy? Blindsiding me like that? Did you think I'd welcome them with open arms, and that we'd all kiss and make up?" She'd kept her voice down on purpose, but her throat hurt from the effort.

"You knew they were coming this weekend," said Kathy. "At the last minute, they changed their plans and took an earlier flight."

"And you didn't think that was important enough to tell me?"

"I think it's important that you make peace with them," replied Kathy.

"You've got that backward. *They* need to make peace with *me!* And with *you.*" Kathy simply didn't get it. "We were children. We were the victims. And I had five extra years alone with them. Five long years. Yes, I've moved on with my life. But I can't pretend those years didn't happen. I don't want peace at any price. You shouldn't, either."

Tonight, she needed a sanctuary.

KATHY'S PHONE CALL the next morning came as no surprise to Heather. She was taking their parents shopping, to get Dad measured for his tuxedo, and a dress for Mom.

"Make sure their charge card hasn't been revoked," said Heather.

"Would you give me a break?"

Heather chuckled.

"The *four* of us are having dinner together tonight. I insist, Heather. I plan to grill steaks on the patio. It'll be more relaxing than at a restaurant."

And less chance of a public scene. "Okay,"

Heather said. "Not that I care about relaxing, but I'll be able to do some behavioral research before the wedding so I can help guarantee you a perfect day."

"They're fine, Heather. I really think you'll be happily surprised. I know I am. They're acting like normal people."

"Sure they are, Kath. Are you going to bring Mark around, take the chance?"

"As a matter of fact," replied Kathy slowly, "we're meeting Mark's parents for dinner tomorrow night."

Heather could say nothing for a moment. "I'll come, too. You might need me."

"No! I—I mean, not 'no.' Of course you're welcome, but not for that reason. These are my parents. I can't pretend otherwise. And I won't live a lie. They'll be who they are, and that's that."

"As long as they're not falling down drunk. But better now than at the wedding," said Heather as she hung up. And better tonight than at the dinner tomorrow.

She glanced at the clock and stood up. The newcomers group would be waiting.

AS HEATHER WALKED into the informal room, Mary Beth was holding up her journal and talking.

"This is working so well for me. It's become more than just a record of my life here. I'm starting to write down the comparison to how I lived at home. Or should I say, prison? Sometimes, there's so much to talk about...look...I'm running out of paper."

"It'll never happen," said Heather lightly, joining the group. "We'll give you as many notebooks as you need."

The woman turned to her, her face pinking up. "Sorry." She sat right down.

"Don't be sorry, Mary Beth. We're here for each other." The group had grown to six. None of the newcomers' abusers came from law enforcement; they might not understand Mary Beth's position.

The newer participants were quiet, simply watching. Mary Beth hadn't gotten to know them yet, but she seemed to be blossoming today.

"Writing in a notebook is a wonderful way to release your emotions. A way to set the record straight." Heather raised her eyes to Mary Beth. "But just as helpful or even better than writing your thoughts down is sharing with other people who've been in similar situations. Are you ready, Mary Beth, to tell us more about Hank? And about your life?"

Heather didn't know what to expect. The flow of

recovery often ran upstream, then down. But Mary Beth had come a long way since she'd been at the shelter.

The woman stood up again and started to pace. "All right. I'll tell you—I'll even show you what it was like to live with a bad cop." She looked at Heather. "I'll be Hank, and you pretend to be me." She flashed a grin, which disappeared just as quickly. "Believe me, you won't have to say much. Here, sit in this chair." She moved a chair so it was by itself, and all the women could see it.

Heather sat down immediately, very encouraged. Role-playing was a powerful tool, and Mary Beth didn't seem afraid to use it.

First, Mary Beth turned her back to the group, but Heather could see her posture change. The woman squared her shoulders. When she faced them again, her eyes were wild, her expression mean and intimidating. She wasn't Mary Beth anymore. She'd transformed herself into Hank Landers. She raised her fist and poured her venom on Heather.

"I'm not going to argue with you…." Her low roar carried a true threat, and Heather felt a jolt run through her.

"Don't make me do this, Mary Beth. When will

you learn to listen to me?" "Hank" shook his fist in Heather's face and leaned over her.

"You idiot! You think you can file charges? Who do you think the cops will believe? Me! They'll believe me. I'll win no matter what it takes."

"No you won't," Heather whispered. "I'm stronger than you. Stronger minded."

"That's a joke." Mary Beth, as Hank, straightened up and swaggered, both hands fisted on her hips. "You have no mind. You're just a whining bitch. So let me tell it to you straight. *We* don't have a problem. *You* have a problem. So *you* go to counseling. *You're* the one who's sick."

Heather interjected, "And I suppose you'll also tell me how I've got it made. Other cops cheat on their wives, drink, do drugs. I'm so lucky to have you." She injected as much sarcasm as she dared without acting too powerful.

"Damn right, you're lucky to have me! You'd never survive without me. Just remember, Mary Beth, this is *my* house, *my* car, *my* money. And these are *my* kids."

Heather started to rise. "Wrong. This is also *my* house, *my* car, *my* money. And these are definitely *my* kids. I'm not stupid, Hank."

"Hank" loomed over Heather, and she fell back in the chair. "Don't mess with me, Mary Beth. I'll kill you if you mess with me or my job."

"Kill me?" Heather whispered. She gripped the armrests. "Do you think you can get away with murder?"

"What do you think? I'm a cop, damn it! I *am* the police. And everyone knows you're crazy."

At that one moment, Heather believed the cop, and she wanted to strangle him. Then Mary Beth stumbled toward the sofa and fell, panting into it. The others were silent, all eyes on the heaving woman.

"Good Lord," whispered Kimberly.

"Amen, sister," said Tashika.

"Mary Beth," said Heather softly, leaning over her on the couch. "You wanted to kill him, didn't you?"

Mary Beth nodded. "Yes, God help me." Tears flowed as the woman sat up and faced Heather. "He's an abusive, worthless piece of dirt, and the thought of him having any kind of custody of the kids…" She shook her head.

"The police brushed the incidents away when Mary Beth reported them," Heather explained to the others.

"It's confusing," said Kimberly, thoughtfully. "The police helped me get out of my situation. They were great…so patient with me…I couldn't have done it without them."

"Which means we shouldn't generalize," said Heather. McCoy flashed in her mind. All six feet of him, with a warm smile just for her. "We've got some dedicated police officers watching out for us right here."

"I know," said Mary Beth. "And that makes me feel better. My problem is that he's still looking for me. And he's bad."

"We're all in that same boat," said Tashika. "We're all scared 'cause our abusers are out there trying to find us." Then she grinned. "The role-playing was great, but I don't believe you really talked back like Ms. Heather was doing." Tashika looked to Heather. "Nice job, counselor."

But Heather disagreed. "If I sounded strong, I did Mary Beth an injustice. She was more frightened in real life than I showed, and that wasn't fair." She paused, her thoughts racing, her heart pounding.

"I have a story to share with y'all today. But it's especially for Mary Beth." She reached for the woman's hand and squeezed it. "When I was growing up, my dad was the Deputy Sheriff of Dry Creek, Texas. And he was the biggest, meanest SOB in the whole town. Everyone called him Big George Marshall because of his size...."

The women stared at her in silence as she spoke. They shivered when she described him. And nodded in recognition at his hammering fists.

And she was committed to having dinner with the man that very evening. She wasn't afraid of him any longer, but she had no intention of making this reunion easy for either George or Jolene.

HANK LANDERS HAD A PLAN for finding Mary Beth and the kids. It was a simple plan, requiring only time and patience. But he was running out of both. His stupid wife didn't know what real trouble was, and when he got his hands on her again, she'd wish for a quick death.

Those same hands tightened on the wheel of his car. *Easy, champ. Easy. Take a breath.*

So far, he'd done everything right. He'd filed a missing persons report as soon as he realized she wasn't coming back. He received the full support of the department and was able to access its resources. His buddies had immediately put the word out among their personal friends in the force all across the city. He'd been given latitude in his work schedule—and the detectives assigned to Mary Beth's case were keeping him up-to-date with their progress. Which was none. Unless they were lying to him.

Most important, he conducted his own investigation. He used the official list of the city's patrols and beats and went out on his own. Like now.

He'd started on the east side, close to his own division, and began to visit the street cops working the beats. They were the guys who knew the neighborhoods—the small safe houses, the larger shelters. He'd come across as a worried man. Hell, it was the truth. His wife was mentally ill, depressed. His kids were at risk, and he needed to find them quickly. The cops sympathized. He even brought along chocolate bars in appreciation. They'd remember him if he came around again.

Mary Beth had left the car. The checkbook. She had no cash, he'd made sure of that. Even her parents didn't know where she was. His mother-in-law started to cry genuine tears. So, Mary Beth had gotten no financial help from them. She and the kids still had to be in town.

At this point, he'd eliminated all the Houston shelters on the east side. His buddies had come up dry so far, no leads, no nothin'. But Hank didn't believe in disappearing acts. And besides, Mary Beth was too dumb to figure one out. Too scared to even try. He'd find her. Three weeks was long enough. She couldn't hide. Not from him.

He stepped on the accelerator and headed for I-10, the Katy Freeway. It might take another three weeks, but he'd work the west side until she was under his roof again.

SHE WOULDN'T MAKE IT easy for them. Heather paid the cashier at Spec's Liquors, satisfied she'd purchased her parents' favorites as well as the Shiraz she and Kathy enjoyed. She was glad Dave hadn't been around when she left the shelter that evening. She definitely didn't want to explain her detour. Her stomach tightened, however, at another thought. If Dave wasn't with her, then he might be on a dangerous call. This was one of the reasons not to become involved with a cop. The work itself triggered problems in the relationship. Not that she and Dave had a relationship—romantically speaking.

She glanced inside the brown paper bag, then set it on the seat next to her. She exhaled deeply. She shouldn't be putting temptation in the way of a couple who'd been sober for two years. If they were telling the truth, it wouldn't be fair to them.

But, it was a big "if," and she didn't care. She knew exactly what she was doing and why, and her reasons had nothing to do with Kathy's wedding. Simply, her anger still simmered. She'd never confronted them and hadn't forgiven George and Jolene. She'd never made them account for her ravaged childhood that had been no childhood at all. For the beatings and the bruises, for making her ashamed to go to school. But most of all, for feeling so powerless. She'd been George's punching bag in the pit.

Ten years away made no difference. Their simple reappearance awakened her resentment. Well, she'd never claimed to be a saint.

Heather let herself in the front door and followed the voices to the back of the house. The kitchen table was set. Kathy and their mother were making a salad at the sink, and George was outside on the patio.

Kathy looked up and smiled. "Just in time, Heather. Glad you're home. Dad is out there lighting the grill. We've got some steaks."

"Sounds great," replied Heather, as she put her package down. She opened an upper cabinet and rooted for the appropriate glasses.

Her dad came in just as she put ice cubes into a

short glass. He stopped when he saw her. "So you came back?"

"Don't feel flattered, George. This is a command appearance for my sister." She lifted the bottle of Jack Daniel's from the bag. "See. I remembered what you like. Want you to feel at home." Kathy gasped. Her dad looked at the other women, confused.

"Doesn't she know about us?" He turned back to Heather. "We're sober now. Look. See." He dug into his pants pocket. "This is my two-year chip from A.A. Mama has one, too."

Heather peered at the proof he'd offered. She knew that Alcoholics Anonymous provided a successful program for those who admitted they were alcoholics. That was the key. No one else could do it for them. She stared at her father—six feet and over two hundred pounds. His five o'clock stubble was half-white, the jowls slack. His eyes, however, were alert. And sane.

"Very nice, George," Heather replied as she opened the whiskey, and splashed two fingers of it over the ice. She lifted the glass and offered it to him. He stepped back, his eyes wide, almost bulging.

"Don't want it now?" asked Heather, placing the drink on the table. "We'll just leave it here in case you change your mind."

"Oh no, we won't," said Kathy, picking it up.

"Leave it!" George's voice still held power, and Kathy paused. "If that's what it takes for her to believe us, then so be it."

Heather poured a similar amount for her mother. "For you, Jolene. Can't play favorites, now, can I? I guess I'm an equal opportunity avenger."

"Do whatever you want, Heather. It won't make a difference." Her mother's voice sounded flat, her expression disappointed.

George walked toward his wife and gave her a hug. "It'll be okay, honey. She'll come around."

Really? "So, Jolene," said Heather, "what did you expect coming here? That I'd fall all over you? Hug you tight like a loving daughter?" It was time to get it all out in the open.

Her mother looked stricken. "But when Kathy invited us to come…I thought…I thought…" Jolene's hands dropped into her lap.

Heather glanced at her sister and saw her telltale color. Her invitation.

"Kathy wasn't around for the worst." Heather moved closer to her mother. "When she left town, you were my only hope. How many times did I beg you for help? You never once protected me from him."

"I couldn't protect myself from him."

"Oh, please," replied Heather. "Don't make excuses. You drank together. And you rutted like animals. So, what do you expect from me now?"

Jolene looked into her eyes and said, "I want another chance, Heather. One more chance."

CHAPTER NINE

ONE MORE CHANCE. Heather tossed in the unfamiliar bed at Welcome Home. Her parents were different from her memories of them. Subdued. Deferential. Sure, they looked older, but ten years would do that to anyone. They were quieter. Their bite was gone.

The two glasses of Jack Daniel's had remained on the table the entire meal. Heather had drunk a full glass of wine, had sipped it slowly, making it last. She'd periodically raised her glass in a toast. To Kathy's happiness. To her parents' continued recovery. To the new van that she'd tried out that day. To anything she could think of. Kathy, disloyal, had chosen to drink a glass of cola, but had raised it in any toast Heather had devised.

Had she not known better, Heather would have thought her parents were an ordinary couple. And then she remembered—they weren't "normal." They were alcoholics. And always would be.

She punched her pillow. If only they had sobered

up twenty years ago, her life would have been so different. So much better. And so would theirs have been. Maybe her dad would have been a good cop like McCoy.

McCoy was a good cop. And a good man. The truth hit her with such force, she held her breath. She rolled over slowly and made herself relax, allowing her thoughts to wander. She liked Dave. She liked his slow smile when he saw her. She was getting used to the man being around and was hoping to see him the next day, hoping he'd donate another Saturday to Girlfriends.

All pretense of sleep deserted her as she imagined herself with Dave McCoy, a lovely slow-motion daydream. Holding hands. Walking in the park under shady trees. She sighed, and reached for more dreams…until a shot rang out. McCoy pushed her to the dirt-packed ground and took off after the perps.

"For cryin' out loud!" Heather switched on the bedside lamp and grabbed a pencil and sheet of paper. Might as well make better use of her time. She started lists for the new shelter. Living with a cop—good one included—was no way to live at all. Not even in her dreams.

DAVE'S PICKUP WAS OUTSIDE Welcome Home the next morning when Heather left the building. She got behind the wheel of the new van, which Gene had loaded with cleaning supplies and gardening tools the previous day. Her own vehicle remained in the parking lot.

She pulled in front of Dave's truck when the gates closed behind her and waited for him. His dark hair curled over his collar and made her fingers itch to run through it. Those unruly waves would be thick and soft and clean and… What was she thinking? Maybe it was time for Sara or Mark to fix her up with someone.

"So why have you slept here the past couple of nights? Has something happened at home?"

Heather had to concentrate. Get her mind off his broad shoulders and how they filled out the jersey he wore.

Sure something had happened. But he didn't have to know about Jolene and George. "Just thought I'd give Kathy privacy. Some time to herself…and Mark."

He started to grin, then paused. "I thought Warner had a big place near the Galleria…." He shrugged. "Ah, well, everyone needs a change."

Heather remained quiet, merely squirmed a bit. She was really getting very skilled at misdirecting people's thoughts.

"By the way," said Dave, "I already picked up bagels and kolaches for breakfast. Juice, too. So, let's get started."

"What? No doughnuts, Officer?"

His grin sent her pulse skyrocketing. "Watch it, lady," he replied. "You're treading on dangerous ground."

An hour later, she'd wished the grounds they'd mowed were less dangerous. Many of the same volunteers had returned as well as some new ones, including her friend, Sara, who now stood on the front porch and yelled inside, "You've got fire ant mounds on the lawn."

Heather hurried to the porch. "Were you bitten?"

Sara shook her head.

"We're taking care of them right now," said Patrick, a bag of ant killer in his hand. "By the end of today, front and back will be treated for insects and weeds. You'll only need weekly mowing and trimming."

Heather gazed at the front yard. "Thanks a lot, Mr. McCoy. You've really helped."

"Isn't that what I'm here for?" He started down the porch steps, then said over his shoulder, "I called your contractor yesterday. He'll ask for me when he gets here. I want to make sure he knows what he's doing."

And suddenly, Heather felt her control of the project slipping away. "I would have gladly included you in my discussions, Mr. McCoy, but please remember that there's only one point man on this project, and that's me."

A familiar McCoy grin slowly crossed his face. "No problem." He went back to what he was doing. Heather's tension dissipated, and she felt silly. She was sure Dave's father knew a thousand percent more about construction than she did. But she was responsible for the funds and was counting on Gene being here to help her with the contractor.

Sara gazed after Patrick. "You'd sure have great-looking kids."

"What?"

"Oh, not him. But his son is the image—" Suddenly, Sara stopped speaking.

Heather glanced up. Her friend's eyes were wide, her mouth gaped. She grabbed Heather's arm and squeezed. "Oh, my God, Heather. Am I seeing things, or is that Kathy with—with—holy moly—with your most loving parents?"

Heather turned her head so fast, she felt dizzy.

"Will you look at that?" continued Sara in amazement. "They actually came all the way to Houston without falling down."

"They're on the wagon," said Heather. "A.A."

Sara shrugged. "It works for some. Not for my happily drinking folks, though."

This was the first time Sara had mentioned her parents in a long while. "Have they tried it?" asked Heather.

"Oh, yeah. Not that it helped. You have to really want to stop drinking for it to work. I guess my folks don't really want to sober up."

"And I," said Heather, "really don't want my folks here." She gave Sara a push. "Why don't you go talk to them for a few hours? Make my life easier. And whatever you do, don't introduce them to the McCoys—father, son or mother, if she shows."

Sara eyed her. "Jolene and George can't influence a guy in love—"

"Sara, forget love. I'm in charge of a whopping amount of money here. I can't let any of these volunteers think I come from an irresponsible family. They'll lose faith in me, and then what will the kids do?"

"Gotcha."

Heather bit her lip as she watched Sara greet George and Jolene and make a big fuss over them. Then she went back inside the first-floor apartment where she'd been pulling up worn-out filthy carpeting. She hoped Kathy would give their parents a quick tour, a sampling of their lives in Houston. She shook her head in disbelief as she thought about how complicated her life had become.

In the past, everything had been simple and manageable: Welcome Home during the day, her Master's program at night and outreach to the kids on alternate evenings. She'd been happily in control.

A tap on the door interrupted her. Sara. "If you don't put Jolene and George to work, the senior McCoy will. From what I can tell, he's organized the whole shootin' match out there."

Heather hurried toward the front of the house.

"Nothing to worry about," continued Sara. "He's a natural leader, and a lot's getting done. He's the kind of person people enjoy working with. Let him direct the group. But your folks want to be a part of it."

Heather was surprised to see Gene talking to Patrick and Dave near the front corner of the building. As if she were a magnet, Dave's eyes were drawn to her. He waved her over and pointed to the side of the house. "We're focusing on the outside only because the inside will be changing. Right now, we're taking down rotten siding and replacing the slats."

"Replacing them? With what? The new siding hasn't been delivered yet."

"I picked up some precut pieces with my truck before I came," said Gene. "Lieutenant McCoy called and said we were ready. And I told the store you'd be in touch with their tax deduction letter for their donation."

When had Patrick and Gene become friendly? When had Gene given out his number? She looked at the faces around her, every one of them beaming with satisfaction. Did it really matter how it happened? *Go with the flow, Heather.*

She smiled at her biggest supporters. "This is great! Thanks so much."

"The mild weather won't last forever," said Dave. "And probably neither will all the volunteers. Let's make every minute count."

"And every person." Kathy added her determined voice to the discussion from where she stood with Jolene and George.

Heather groaned silently, and inclined her head toward the door. "Inside," she said, without making introductions. "We've got plenty of work. Inside." She stared pointedly at her sister, and Kathy nodded. Her parents seemed delighted.

She led the trio to a back bedroom she hadn't gotten to yet. "I'm lifting carpeting," she said. "It's hard work and dusty. And I'm sure you didn't come to Houston to clean a house, so I can give you a tour of the place, and you can enjoy the rest of the day. Somewhere else."

"Nope. This is where we want to be," said her dad.

"With you." Jolene's soft voice beseeched her daughter.

Damn it. Heather avoided her mother's eyes and instead checked the time. Ten-thirty. They wouldn't last more than thirty minutes doing hard work.

She knelt on the floor and used a screwdriver as a lever to pry the carpeting up. After she got it started, she stood and gave the tool to George. "Here you go. When the whole perimeter is up, you can use the razor in the other room to cut the rug into strips."

She returned to the front porch where Dave met her. "The contractor's asking for you."

Dave went with her to join Gene and Patrick who were already with the man. The five of them took an hour's tour while the contractor made notes about breaking through and connecting the top-floor apartments, taking out three kitchens, knocking down walls, preserving beams. The man talked. The other three nodded. Heather said nothing until the end of their inspection, when they were all on the wide front porch again.

"How much money? And how much time?" she

asked, notebook, calendar and calculator in hand. She'd included an estimate in her grant, but this was the real thing.

"It's the time that might get you," said Gene. "The teardown needs to be done before the volunteers can really make the place shine. And your contractor will need help knocking down the walls."

She looked down at her calendar just as Anne McCoy approached. "We've got pizza for lunch today," said Anne, nodding toward her car.

"That's where I come in," said Patrick.

"For pizza?"

The retired cop laughed, walked toward his ex-wife and kissed her on the cheek. "That, too. No, for remodeling." He looked at Heather. "I've got the most time, and if I help this professional," he said, nodding at the contractor, "we should get the job done pretty quickly."

"I'm not too bad a hand, either," said Dave.

"You?" asked Patrick. "I thought you were studying for the sergeant exam. That's what you need your spare time for. You don't want to mess up your career."

"Damn stupid career," murmured Anne.

Standing alongside her, Heather jerked with surprise and watched Patrick's expression harden for a moment. "What?" she whispered, but the woman simply shook her head.

Dave, however, stared at his father. "I can organize my own life, Dad."

"Absolutely right," said Anne. "A well-balanced life is best. Part work, part play."

Heather felt the undercurrents as strongly as if she were caught in a riptide. Time to change the subject.

"Pizza sounds wonderful, but it's too expensive for you, Mrs. McCoy. I'll pay you for it." Oops. The woman glared at her. "Or," Heather amended, "at least, let me split it with you."

"It's my contribution. Don't worry about it. And when it's time to decorate, I'm your gal."

"Think inexpensive," said Heather. "As in cheap. And easy to clean. Machine wash."

Anne grinned. "Bring it on. The bigger the challenge, the better I like it."

"That's because you're stubborn," said Patrick. "When you're committed to something, you don't give up until it's right. Even now."

The older couple eyed each other. An awkward silence fell on the group. "I knew when to fold," Anne whispered. "At least I thought I did. I thought I'd cut my losses and gain some sanity. Maybe I was wrong."

"Or maybe I was," said Patrick.

"Aw, hell!" said Dave. "Do we have to have a live melodrama in front of an audience?"

Then, out of the corner of her eye, Heather saw her dad come through the apartment door with large carpet remnants in his arms. Rivulets of sweat rolled from his temples. He proceeded outside, dropped the carpet in the corner of the porch, and blotted his face before he turned to her.

"Heather, girl," he said excitedly. "The bedroom floors are bare. Do you know what's there? What was underneath that filthy rug?"

"No clue, George." As if her dad ever cared about floors in the pit. Or about anything.

"Beautiful wood," he replied. "Oak. That's going to be one hell of a floor when this house is done, or my name isn't Big George Marshall."

Heather sighed, saw her mom and Kathy in the doorway, and glanced at Dave. "Did you say, melodrama? Here comes Act II."

SO THAT WAS HEATHER'S DAD. Not what Dave had expected. Not that he'd thought about her parents much. Somehow, Heather and Kathy had always seemed like a self-contained family unit. Although his name seemed to fit him, Big George Marshall didn't carry himself like a powerhouse. In fact, he seemed a bit timid around Heather. And her mother even more so. How did these two ever produce the confident girl he was falling in love with?

He waited for Heather to introduce them, but it was Kathy who filled in the gap. A prewedding visit. Shopping in the big city. Reconnecting with their daughters. Dinner tonight with Kathy and Mark and Mark's parents. It sounded logical, but he knew Heather well enough to read her body language. She was uncomfortable dealing with her parents.

He walked around his mother and took Heather's arm, drawing her aside. "What's wrong, Heath?"

She wrinkled her nose. "It's complicated."

"That's nothing new. We're human. You think my folks are easy to figure out? I love them, yet they can still drive me nuts—if I let them."

"You, my friend, are one up on me. Any love I had for mine was beaten out of me long ago."

She sounded like a little girl, her voice trailing off very small and quiet. Then her words sank in. *Beaten?* She'd been beaten as a kid? He wrapped his arms around her and just held her. He wanted to protect her. And love her.

And then he'd take care of "big" George Marshall.

He nuzzled Heather's ear and whispered her name, saw the pink color her cheeks. Light complexions always revealed the truth, and Heather was definitely not immune to him.

Suddenly, the air around them got quiet, and the hairs on the back of his neck seemed to stand up. He turned and saw two pairs of eyes staring at them. He squared his shoulders as he looked first at his mom, then at his dad. "What?" he challenged.

His mother's mouth made a small circle. "Ooh. Uh. How about some pizza?" asked Anne. Not a bad save.

Then George's voice joined in. "Heather, why don't you introduce us to your boyfriend?"

The pink in her cheeks quickly turned bright red. Dave could feel the instant heat through her clothes.

"Act III," he whispered, and squeezed her lightly. He extended his hand. "Dave McCoy, HPD, and Heather's friend. A close friend."

"I'm Heather's dad. Used to be in law enforcement in our hometown. I liked it."

"Retired, like me?" asked Patrick amiably.

George smiled and nodded, then a film seemed to cover his expression. "Something like that."

Heather was as still as a cat eyeing a mouse. "Is

that what they teach you in those monthly meetings you go to, George? How to dress up the truth?"

"Heather!" Kathy broke in, horrified. "Please."

Dave's brain clicked into gear as he gazed from George to Heather and back again. He connected the dots between words spoken and words left unsaid.

"Some cops do drink too much, but they don't all wind up in A.A. Congratulations," said Dave. "Wise choice."

"Traitor," whispered Heather, poking him in the ribs.

"Too much melodrama," he whispered back. "With you in the starring role."

Sighing, she said, "Maybe so. Sometimes, I really should tape my mouth shut. Want to go to dinner at a fancy country club tonight?"

She didn't have to ask him twice.

"THAT YOUNG MAN is courting you." Jolene stood in the doorway of Heather's workout room. She wore a navy-blue pant suit with a fitted red jersey tucked inside the waistband, and a pair of low-heeled navy shoes. She looked neat and clean, but could have been going to work at a downtown law firm.

"You need some jewelry to dress up your outfit," said Heather. "Something around your neck. Ask Kathy. I don't own any."

Jolene was quiet for a moment, then smiled so widely her eyes crinkled shut. "Okay. I'll ask her. I want to look as pretty as I can for—for Mark's family…and…and…oh, never mind."

"What are you worried about, Jolene? George can't take his eyes off you."

Her mother brushed the comment aside. "Your daddy's always been crazy about me. That was never the problem." She took a deep breath. "And Mark loves your sister. We saw that when they visited us last year. We'd only been sober about six months, but the visit worked out real well."

"I guess so," said Heather, shimmying into a black sleeveless dress. "Mark stuck around."

"We like him a lot. He's a good person. And so is your Dave McCoy. That's what I really wanted to say."

Did Jolene actually think her opinion mattered? "I imagine you thought Daddy was a 'good person' when you married him."

"Your daddy is a fine person," Jolene insisted. "But he has a disease. And I've got the same one."

The medical community had distinguished alcoholism as a disease. Heather, the teenager, had called the explanation a cop-out.

Now she looked at her mother. "You have the disease, but I was also a victim. Can you give me back my childhood, Mama? Can you make the years disappear and live them over with kindness and, at the very least, normalcy?"

Jolene leaned against the door frame as if to support herself, but she didn't step back. "You know the answers to those questions, Heather. Ask for the possible, not the impossible. For me, the possible lies in looking forward. In not using alcohol in any form. That's what I can do. That's the only way this particular disease can be arrested. Not cured, but arrested."

Was this the same woman who'd spent fifty years without a backbone? Who'd enabled her husband to drink, and then joined him in getting blitzed? Who ignored the effects on her children?

Heather studied her mother closely. Jolene stood perfectly still.

"Sobriety looks very nice on you, Jolene. Keep it up."

Her mother's natural smile lightened her face, made her seem younger. "One day at a time." She turned to go back to the others.

Heather walked toward her. "Hang on a sec… If George ever falls off the wagon, I suggest you run like hell."

"You know what, Heather? That's exactly what I told him about me. 'Run like hell, Georgie,' I said, 'cause I'll bring you right back down again.'"

It seemed her parents were in this life together, for better or worse, even if the worse was strictly their own doing.

Not her problem.

FIVE MINUTES AFTER Kathy, Mark and her parents left the house that evening, the doorbell rang.

"You look incredible," said Dave as soon as she opened the door.

Actually, if anyone looked incredible, it was Dave. Heather couldn't stop staring. His big dark eyes, and that wavy hair… He was wearing a charcoal-gray suit with a pin-striped gray-on-gray shirt and solid tie. He looked…so, so… If she didn't stop staring at him, she'd melt right there.

"I don't think I need a wrap," she said.

It took him a second, but then his laughter filled the hallway. He moved closer, and his lips covered hers as naturally as if they'd found home. His kiss was slow and deliberate, his tongue traced the outline of her mouth. She shivered. His familiar spicy aftershave, which she recognized now, added to her hunger, and she returned his kiss eagerly.

"Heather?" he finally whispered, his voice gravelly. "What are we doing? What do you want?"

She was on fire. As soon as she'd seen him. She shook her head to clear it, for sanity's sake, barely able to meet his glance. "What is it with us? With you?" she replied in a low voice. "It's been years since anyone's affected me this way...."

His grin, that slow sexy grin, had her reeling. And this time, she couldn't blame it on a near-death experience.

"For starters," he replied, "the word slow doesn't seem to be in our vocabulary. And that's a first for me, too."

Maybe. "I know better than that," she replied. "Cops always have a few groupies hanging around. It's the uniform thing."

"Not true at all," he replied. "The only people I see in groups are the pushers, the prostitutes and the users."

"Really?"

He kissed her lightly. “Really.”

She grabbed her purse. “Ready?”

“I certainly am.”

CHAPTER TEN

"JUST LOOK AT THIS PLACE," Heather said as she and Dave drove through the grounds of the Emerald Oaks Country Club. The distance from the state road to the club entrance was almost a half mile. "It looks like a plantation."

Dave chuckled. "I think it was actually modeled on a Bermuda plantation. In any case, golf courses require land, and the club also has a dozen tennis courts and three swimming pools."

"And you know so much because you're a secret member?" Heather knew full well a cop's salary didn't stretch far enough for a membership here.

"More like security detail when I want extra cash." He glanced at her. "But would you be impressed if I were?"

He had to be kidding. "Hardly. I'd think you'd be an idiot to go into debt…oh, oh, look, there's a deer right off the road in that stand of trees." The deer lifted its head and stared at the passing car. "Aw… such big beautiful eyes. So delicate."

"And here I thought you were a hardened city girl," said Dave, "but you're still a sucker for Bambi."

"I'm a city girl through and through. Had enough country to last a lifetime. But, this is so peaceful." Her hometown had been mostly brown, just as its name implied. Dry Creek. Brown and harsh. Residents fought to raise a green lawn next to their houses. Her yard, of course, had been pure dirt.

Dave pointed ahead to the large brick-and-glass building, light from its windows creating a warm glow. He pulled around the circular driveway to the front door and nodded at the valet for service.

"We can park it ourselves…" Heather began. But Dave shook his head.

"Not tonight," he said quietly. "Let tonight be special. Let's consider this our first official date." He took her arm, tucking it inside his.

His tender expression silenced her. And his eagerness for this so-called date, well, it was irresistible.

"Okay," she whispered. "You're on. But it would be a lot easier to enjoy the night if I could forget why I'm really here."

He brushed a kiss across her temple. "You're

really here with me, and your folks will be fine. They won't want to disappoint Kathy. So, feel free to lighten up."

They entered the club, and a maître d' appeared in front of them as if by magic, before Heather could absorb the elegant decor of the large foyer.

"The Warner family party," said Dave to the man, and Heather was reminded that Kathy's name would soon change, and country club memberships would become part of her life. Keeping pace with the hostess who escorted them to the main dining room, they arrived just as Mark, Kathy and the four parents were being seated at a round table.

"Perfect timing." Mark stood up again, as did his father, Charles Warner, who Heather recognized from having met him once. Tall, trim, with steel-gray hair, he exuded the confidence of a successful man. His firm handshake reinforced the impression.

Then Heather greeted his wife, Vivian, whose perfect appearance bespoke hairdressers, makeup techniques and hours in the gym…or on the tennis courts. She not only looked fabulous for her age, she looked fabulous, period. Except for…her smile. Something wasn't right. Heather studied the other woman. Tonight, Vivian's smile seemed forced.

Heather and Dave sat across from Kathy and Mark while the two sets of parents sat opposite each other. The table was set with white linen cloths and lovely gold-plated dinnerware. Heather looked around the table, observing the other couples, and thinking how well matched they all seemed. Perhaps her parents were too well matched. Maybe with other mates…

"The champagne is chilled, sir," the waiter said to Charles. "Would you like it brought now?"

Well, that didn't take long. Heather glanced across the table. Kathy looked nervous. She seemed about to speak when George said, "We sure want to toast the children's happiness, Charles."

Now, Heather's stomach tightened. Just when she'd started to believe in a miracle, was her dad going to throw it away?

But George surprised her. He looked at the waiter. "If you've got some club soda with a twist of lime for my wife and me, that would be better." He turned toward Mark's dad. "Thanks. But the doc said to lay off the booze if we want to live long enough to see grandchildren."

"And we surely do want that," added Jolene.

"The doctor said that…to both of you?" Vivian's

sharp voice rose in question. She glanced from Jolene to George and back again, eyes narrowing.

"Yes, ma'am," George replied.

"Oh, dear. I knew something wasn't right. We should have met long before today." Her glance rested on Mark. "Just what has our son gotten into?"

"Vivian!" Charles Warner's tone combined warning and exasperation.

The woman's eyes flashed, and her mouth snapped shut. She nodded. "Very well. For now."

Her warning reverberated around the table. The subject would be reopened.

Kathy seemed frozen, her complexion as pale as parchment. Heather, on the other hand, could feel her body heat approach boiling point. She shifted slightly in her chair and eyeballed Mark's mother. But before she could say anything, Mark stood up and brought Kathy with him. He stroked her face. His hand trembled. "I adore you," he said. "I love you with all my heart." And he kissed her in a way that left no doubt about his feelings.

Heather put two fingers in her mouth and whistled loudly, country club be damned. Dave tapped his water glass with his fork which emitted a ringing sound. Soon Jolene and George did the same. The people at the surrounding tables started to applaud. The sound must have penetrated, because Mark lifted his head, surprise etched on his face. Then he grinned. A big bear of a grin.

"We're getting married!" he announced in a voice that swept the room. "Champagne and dessert for everyone, on me!" The response was more than Heather could have imagined. The whole stately dining room broke into applause and congratulations. Some people came over to chat with the couple. Kathy began to laugh and mingle, back to her normal self, which was all Heather wanted to see.

She glanced toward Vivian whose smile remained in place while she greeted friends who had no idea what had transpired prior to Mark's announcement. The woman was trained to play her part. A moment later, Heather got up. She wasn't through with Mrs. Warner.

Dave whispered, "Don't pull her hair out in public."

Hair pulling wouldn't be painful enough. She approached the other woman when the last well-wisher had gone. "Your son," she said, not giving Mark's mother a chance to escape, "was fortunate enough to fall in love with my sister, a woman who's pure gold." Heather picked up a dish from the table and pointed to the design. "Not gold plate that loses luster like this. You are extremely lucky to have Katherine in your family. I advise you not to blow it, or you might be left wondering what your grandchildren look like."

The woman blanched. "Which, of course," Heather added, "would be Mark's doing because he's devoted to Kathy…and would want to protect her from you." She turned and left the woman standing alone.

"Mrs. Warner looks ill," said Dave, rising when Heather approached. "What did you tell her?"

"Oh, nothing important." Heather waved her hand with an airy motion. "Just a little something about never seeing her grandchildren."

He whistled long and low. "Show no mercy. 'Atta girl."

"Oh, let the woman stew. She deserves it."

He raised his hands in a gesture of defeat. "No argument there."

Heather moved closer to him and tilted her head up. "What's more," she whispered, "her husband heard every word I said and didn't interrupt."

"Well, he's sure speaking to her now."

Sure enough, Dave was right. "I hope his words are effective," she said. "Kathy deserves every happiness."

"Only Kathy?" Dave asked quietly, his arms around her. "What about you?" His glance lingered on her face, his eyes dark with feeling.

She didn't know what to say. "What a question." She laughed self-consciously. "I don't know. I…I…guess I'm already happy."

"There's nothing missing? Nothing more you want?" Dave reached for her hand. "Come on. I'll show you."

Heather looked around. A number of people had left their tables and were dancing in the adjoining room. "I never noticed the dancing."

"You were distracted." He led her to the dance floor and slipped his arms around her. She leaned against him, felt his lips brush against her hair, heard him sigh. "Heather…Heather…"

She understood. Nodded her head against his chest. "Yeah. This is nice."

And it was. He held her, but not too hard, as though she were precious to him. Her thoughts flowed and wandered. Slow dancing was a great invention. Just the two of them in their own private world. No parents. No work issues. Nothing but the music and the dancing. Getting used to each other. His strong back and hard chest. Did he feel her softness against him?

She felt his hand travel slowly down her spine and pause where her hips started to flare. She heard him inhale sharply. Felt the tempo of his heart quicken. Then, just as his hand had done, her palm made lazy circles on his back, little by little drifting lower down to his waist…enjoying the play, enjoying the exploration…until she bumped into something hard. And the mood vanished.

"You're carrying!"

"WHY DON'T YOU JUST ELOPE?" Heather asked later that night, sitting on Kathy's bed watching her pack a few items. "It seems to me families make things harder."

Mark was in the kitchen waiting and visiting with George and Jolene, who'd had a wonderful evening. Kathy had decided to go with Mark—to calm him down. Despite Vivian's apology, he was still very upset. Or maybe anxious to reinforce that she was his one and only.

"If it were simply a matter of Mark and me, we'd escape in a minute. I certainly have no family to insult by not having a big wedding. And while Mark's family is much larger, half the guests will be business people. It's important to Mark and his dad. I'm not going to interfere with that."

Heather shrugged. "I'd elope."

But Kathy shook her head. "Sometimes, you do what's best in the long run. What's best for your husband's career. Just think of my wedding as networking," she said. "His dad started the business, and Mark's dedicated to it."

"Just as long as he's dedicated to you."

Kathy's grin lit up the room. "I don't think he's through raging at his mom yet, but I'll handle her from now on. She simply took me by surprise tonight. I'd thought she was coming around in recent months, getting used to the idea that Mark didn't fall in love with a society girl. I guess our folks shook her sensibilities. I'll give Vivian credit for a beautiful apology, but she won't catch me off guard again."

"A beautiful apology, huh? How beautiful?" Nothing less than genuine tears would do for Heather.

Kathy raised her eyebrows. "Very heartfelt, I think. A bit embarrassed of course. But, yes, I think it was sincere. She wants peace and love in the family, too."

Heather gave her sister a hug. "You're still such an idealist."

Kathy put her hands on Heather's shoulders. "Without hope, Heather, what have we got?"

BY THE TIME HEATHER arrived in the kitchen, Kathy and Mark had gone. Her parents were chatting quietly with Dave. "Will you two be all right here by yourselves?"

Her dad started. "Aren't you going to stay?"

Heather couldn't decide if he wanted her company, or simply felt uncomfortable in new surroundings. "You both did great tonight. I know it must have been difficult with the champagne everywhere."

"Not too hard, honey," said Jolene. "And worth every minute."

"Champagne was never our beverage of choice," added her father. His eyes sought the cabinet where Heather had put the whiskey she'd bought the night before. "Now, Jack Daniel's…well, that's another story."

Heather couldn't believe what she was hearing. "Tempted, George?"

"Every day," he said. "But I haven't touched a drop in two years. Two years."

Dave's gaze shifted from one to the other, then he crossed the room. "And you won't be touching it tonight." He took the whiskey out of the cabinet. "Anything else in the house?"

She got the wine from the fridge. "That's it."

"Leave them!" George boomed. "I'm not a child. And no one said this was easy." Perspiration trickled down his face.

"But no one said make it harder than it has to be," Jolene replied quickly. She stood before her husband, a hand on his cheek. "What are you trying to prove, Georgie? Right now, Heather doesn't matter. Only the next hour matters." She appealed to Dave. "I'll pour both bottles down the toilet if you leave them here. Save your money. Take them."

"Yes, ma'am. Come on, Heather. I'll give you a ride to the shelter." It was an order, not a question.

But her feet were rooted. Her parents were still a team, but now playing for a different league. "Why?" she whispered. "What happened that caused you to try?"

Her dad lifted his gaze to her. "Short version—I was driving drunk with Mama in the car. I crashed, and she wound up in the hospital. Broken ribs, broken arm. Internal bleeding. I went to jail. Couldn't make bail. Couldn't visit her. I almost lost her." He looked over her shoulder, out at the dark night. "I almost lost my Jo." His gravelly voice trailed off. "But worst of all, I couldn't remember any of it. And that's when I knew."

He shook his head. "Come on, Jo. I'm tired."

It was Jolene who saw Heather and Dave out the door. “We’ll be fine.”

“For now,” said Heather.

“That’s right,” Jolene replied. “And *now* is what I care about.”

She closed the door, and Heather and Dave stood outside without speaking while they listened to the lock turn. They ambled toward their vehicles.

“They shouldn’t have had children.”

Dave stopped and gently pulled her to him. “I’m grateful they did.”

“But you don’t know…” Her voice choked, and she blinked to prevent tears from falling.

“Oh, I think I can guess,” said Dave softly, nuzzling her neck. “I’ve seen the human condition in all its forms—the best and the worst. But mostly, I’ve seen the worst.”

She imagined a cop usually did. “That’s some job you have.”

“Don’t throw stones, my girl.” He nibbled her earlobe and whispered, “You survived them. That’s what matters.”

She relaxed against him. She had survived. And done well.

“You’re strong,” he added. “I like that you fight for what you’re doing, what you believe in.”

His approval warmed her.

"…as long as you use good judgment."

Instantly, she put more space between them to see his expression. "According to whose point of view?"

"Is there any question?" he asked in mock surprise. "Mine, of course." He put the two bottles in his truck, then opened the passenger door for her.

"I'm working at Girlfriends tomorrow. I can take my own car."

He shook his head. "Nah. It's late. I'll pick you up in the morning, and I'll put in a few hours at the place. Can't refuse an offer like that, can you?"

Well, no. "Pretty clever, Officer."

He chuckled. "I'm sneaky when necessary."

His fingers skimmed her jawline, and she nuzzled his hand. Then she reached up to caress his cheek. A full moon provided pale light, and all around them, it was quiet. She saw the tenderness in Dave's eyes and something more, something exciting, but tempered. Want? Passion? There would be time to find out. Now, she enjoyed the peacefulness between them. The comfort. Until Dave whispered, "I'd put my life on the line for you, Heather. I hope you know that."

Her heart pounded. She pushed away from him. "Don't say that. Please. Don't scare me. I don't want anyone's life in danger because of me."

"Shh... Shh. It's just my way of saying I...uh...care about you." He kissed the corner of her mouth. "Very, very much. I guess I'm used to that expression."

She heard what he'd almost said. Was glad he'd changed the verb. Love. God, that was a strong word. It could be wonderful, of course. But it also made people act crazy. Like her parents. Love and dependency. Sick. She worked with dependent women every day, helping them find confidence and learn the skills they needed to rely only on themselves. She'd never put herself in a situation where she'd depend on any man for survival. But here was Dave, offering himself up, talking about *his* life.

"Slow down," she said. "You've already put yourself out there for me. I've gotten my fair share of Dave McCoy's personal lifesaving service. So you can stop now. And take care of yourself."

His kiss came quick and hard. Then he opened the passenger-side door for her. "In you go, sweetheart."

Despite her reservations, she liked the sound of "sweetheart." He'd called her that several times now. He was clearly making his feelings known to her, which made her feel special. Maybe because she really liked him. But... Somehow, there was always a but. *Go with your heart, Heather.* You already trust him. Just go for it.

Walking through the halls of Welcome Home a few minutes later, she thought about each woman in the shelter as she passed her door. Beaten up but not beaten down. Every one of them looking for help. By the time Heather reached her temporary apartment, she realized how ignorant she was about the one person who affected her life the most: herself. While her clients hung on her every word, she was afraid to follow her own advice.

"Maybe this is the part where some girls talk to their moms," she murmured. "And others simply flounder until they learn to trust themselves."

THE NEXT MORNING, Dave waited at McDonald's drive-up window while the clerk filled two large cups of coffee. He knew how Heather liked hers—with milk, not cream, and a pack of sweetener on the side. Two boxes of doughnuts and a gallon of juice rested on the seat next to him. She'd appreciate the gesture. Most guys brought a woman flowers or candy. Or took her out to dinner. Heather, of course, was not most women. He'd win her over with doughnuts or kolaches or pizzas or whatever it took to feed her volunteer crew.

Heather put her heart into her work, establishing a home for girls. Girls, just like the girl she'd once been. After meeting her parents, he understood exactly why she did what she did.

He thanked the clerk, took a sip of his coffee and drove to pick her up. He wasn't disappointed. Her eyes glowed when she climbed into the truck and saw the sweets. Her smile sent him into orbit. "God, you're beautiful." He breathed the words without a second thought.

"You need glasses?" she asked, shaking her head. "I'm dressed for work. Not a smear of makeup. But thanks a lot. I guess. And big thanks for the doughnuts." She reached for her coffee and lifted the cap, lowered her face to inhale. "Oh, the first cup's always the best. I don't suppose you brought—"

"The sweetener's on the seat somewhere."

"This is perfect."

He pulled onto the road and drove to the Girlfriends site. He wished they were taking a long ride out in the country somewhere. Just by themselves. "Guess we're not the first ones here," he said. "There's my dad, Kathy, Mark and your folks. Dad must be excited about your project."

"And I thought my family would all sleep in." She sounded disappointed.

As he parked the truck, Dave said, "Seems like George did have a rough night. He looks tired."

She shrugged as if she didn't care. But he saw her forehead crease. "As long as his eyes aren't bloodshot from booze."

He didn't comment. His own father had walked a thin line, too. It was one of the reasons for the divorce. Patrick had fallen into the habit of relaxing with the boys too often. Way too often. Until it had become routine and his mom couldn't take it anymore. Those were rough days. He didn't like thinking about them.

"Mark's been generous to us," said Heather. "But this is the first time he's been down here."

They climbed out of the truck and Dave shook Warner's hand. "Ready to roll up your sleeves, oilman?"

"That and more." Mark turned to Heather and gave her a hug. "I like a woman who speaks her mind. And I especially like the woman who thinks I'm the luckiest man alive—because of Kathy. So, come on and give me a proper tour of this place, this dream you have. Maybe I can help make it come true a little faster."

Dave watched Heather as Mark's words sank in. Then she glanced at him with a question in her eyes. He understood. She didn't quite believe what she was hearing. He nodded. "I think you've just gotten your first benefactor."

"All right!" She took out the key and motioned to Mark. "Come on, Mr. Philanthropist, you might even have some ideas..." Their voices faded away, and Dave turned toward Kathy and the others.

"You okay?"

"Oh, yes. Definitely." She couldn't stop smiling.

"They don't come better than my daughters," said George. His glance followed his future son-in-law. "His old lady will come around. She's blind, not stupid."

Jolene nodded. "She's a mother. She wants him to be happy. That's—that's the important thing. That the children be happy."

To Dave's surprise, Jolene started to cry.

"I think...I think," she stuttered, "that Heather will be happy when we go home. She doesn't really want us here."

Dave looked around for an escape, but there was no place to hide outdoors. He was as brave as the next guy, but this was out of his league. As if by telepathy, a blue-and-white car rolled up and his buddy, Powers, got out. Dave covered a lot of ground in very little time.

"Looking for me? Need some assistance?" Powers would think he was crazy.

But the other cop simply shook his head. “Nope. But our karate kid might.”

Dave felt his adrenaline surge. He was on-duty, even if it was his day off.

CHAPTER ELEVEN

THE COPS ON THE WEST SIDE were idiots. Hank Landers got back into his car after showing his badge to an Officer Powers, working his beat. What was there in, “Help me find my depressed wife and two kids?” that Powers couldn’t understand? The guy barely heard him. Maybe his mind was on other things. But not when Hank needed information. He gave the cop a chocolate bar anyway. This disgrace-to-the-uniform would need a reminder of Hank Landers.

Hank gunned the engine and started criss crossing streets. Man, it had been a bad morning. He rotated his shoulder carefully and winced. It still hurt from the fall he took in the kitchen when he slipped on the puddle of last night’s beer. Mary Beth would have plenty to keep her busy after he found her. No more disappearing acts.

He glanced at a list of addresses he’d researched, addresses of the bigger shelters. He’d prefer to visit with a local cop at his side. He knew how protective these places were. The staff wouldn't give up anyone or anything, and they usually had reliable security in place. But if he went with someone they trusted—someone who also trusted him—he could get very, very lucky.

He slowed the car to a crawl. Strange for a Sunday. There were a whole bunch of people fixing up a building. Maybe the local preacher told them to clean up the place, to give back to the community. He shrugged. A bunch of do-gooders.

As he pulled closer, he studied the scene more carefully. Suddenly, he began to grin. A couple of those guys were cops. Sure, they were out of uniform, but he could make a cop with his eyes closed. Hank parked his car, got out and strolled toward the action. The older guy, who was in good shape, bent down to tie his shoe, then turned his head just enough for his glance to focus on Hank. It was an old tried-and-true method for buying time while keeping a low profile. Oh, yeah. Hank was in luck today. This place was crawling with cops.

PATRICK KNEW ABOUT Officer Powers's visit and his heads-up to Dave. He didn't really know if the cop's missing wife and kids were staying at Welcome

Home, and he didn't think it mattered. The effectiveness of all the shelters could hinge on the safety of one woman in one program.

At the same time, if these victims were at Welcome Home, he'd prefer to get rid of the guy before Heather came outside again. He glanced around for his son, glad Dave was hammering in more siding. He had been about to help him, but chose to meet their visitor first.

The man approached with one hand outstretched and the other pulling out his badge as he spoke. "I'm guessing you belong to the same organization?"

Patrick nodded. "Retired."

"Good enough. I won't beat around the bush. I need some help."

Patrick listened while Landers told his story. Then he suggested all the obvious resources: missing persons report, charge cards, bus stations, airplane tickets, girlfriends, relatives…everything that a television show like *Law and Order* would have featured.

"Did it. Did it. Did it."

Patrick shook his head. "Then I'm probably not going to be much help. I haven't patrolled a beat in more than twenty years. But I can spread the word." He started walking toward the other man's car.

"What're y'all doing here?" asked Landers, who

paused to look at the building and watch the elder Marshalls drag more carpeting outside.

"Renovating an old house," Patrick replied.

"I can see that." Landers said impatiently. "What for?"

Stick to the truth—sort of. "It's going to be some kind of a kids' center. After-school stuff, or maybe a day care center."

"Waste of money, if you ask me. Make the mothers stay home and you won't need any day care centers. Hell, my kids never went to one."

Patrick took another step toward the curb.

"Hey, Dad," Dave said.

Damn! But Patrick smiled and faced his son. "What's up?" he asked, looking at the siding in Dave's hand, and hoping Dave would leave quickly.

Too much to hope for.

"Dave, this is Officer Hank Landers."

"HPD," supplied Landers. "You?"

Dave nodded as he studied the other man.

"Figured. You and your dad—two peas in a pod. My boy and I…we're the same way."

"Landers," repeated Dave, as though tasting the word.

Patrick watched as his son transitioned from an

animated construction worker to a police officer covered in image armor. No expression. No emotion. The working face of a cop on duty where feelings must be suppressed. For the first time, Patrick was an observer. Anne had been right. Cops were two different people in one body. How many times had he come home still wearing that armor, unable to separate his two identities?

And his son would go through the same thing. But at what cost? Surprised at the pain he felt, he didn't allow his thoughts to show.

"Officer Landers is looking for some help." Patrick quickly reiterated what they already knew.

Dave held on to the piece of siding. "I'll remember," he said.

"Thanks," said Landers. "And one more thing. Can you check out the shelters on your beat? In case she was wandering, you know, and they took her in."

That was the lamest thing Patrick had ever heard. A shelter would have called an ambulance if a woman was sick. This was a cop with no imagination.

"Sure, man," said Dave. "No problem."

"There's a big one called Welcome Home," said Landers, staring at Dave. "It's on my list. You know it?"

"I do," replied Dave, not offering more.

Tell him you'll check it out. Let's get rid of him. Patrick's mind raced, even as Heather ran toward their little group. Damn, she was there.

"Dave! You'll never guess—" She halted. "Oh, sorry to interrupt."

Landers lit up when he saw her, but quickly banked his interest and offered a casual nod. Patrick glanced at his son. Dave's armor was gone. His eyes burned. His normally calm and controlled son wanted to take the man down.

LANDERS WAS SCUM. Dave hefted the board he held, itching to slam it against Landers's head, but choosing to protect Heather from the man's direct gaze. He moved partially in front of her, then shifted sideways to look into her face. She didn't know about Officer Powers's visit, that Powers had given them a heads-up about Landers.

"Heather." He spoke her name sharply, saw her surprise and curiosity. He stared hard. Would she get the message?

"Yes?" she asked calmly.

"This man is looking for his wife. He's a cop and..." That's all it took for him to transform her into a piece of sculpture. She stood immobile.

"My wife's sick," said the cop, stepping closer. "The docs say she's clinically depressed. She took my kids, and now I'm worried. And scared, too."

If her complexion got any paler, she'd pass out.

"I'm sorry for your troubles," said Heather, turning to leave. "Have you tried the hospitals?"

"No luck," Landers replied. "So now I'm trying the women's shelters. I think that's a reasonable bet…but I'm not sure a woman would take two kids to a place like that."

She paused. "Depended if she needed a sanctuary, now wouldn't it? But there's no accounting for mental illness, Officer…? Sorry, I didn't get your name."

"Landers," he replied. "John Henry Landers. I go by Hank."

Dave tasted her fear. If he'd had any question regarding the whereabouts of Mrs. Landers and her children, he now had the definitive answer.

"Sorry, Officer Landers, I can't help you," said Heather. "As you can see, we're under construction here. And this shelter is for teenagers."

"Shelter?" he asked, looking at Dave, his eyes narrowing. "I thought it was an after-school center."

Dave shrugged. Who had told him that? "It's for kids." *Wanna make something of it?*

Landers pulled a pad from his back pocket. "Okay, okay. Keep your shirt on. But now we're getting somewhere." He looked at Heather. "You probably know the places my wife would go around here. I don't know the west side so well. Who runs the one called Welcome Home?"

Heather looked straight at him. "I'm really sorry, Officer. I know how worried you are, but I don't know. My work is with teenagers. Mobile outreach. I work from my van." She shrugged, a gesture so innocent, so ingenuous, Dave worked to keep his astonishment in check.

"But if I hear anything—" she gestured airily "—from on the streets and all, I'll surely let you know." Then she smiled at the cop. A cute, ingenuous smile, and Dave wanted to hug her and kill her at the same time.

She gracefully extended her hand. "Do you have a business card, Officer Landers?"

In Landers's eagerness, five cards dropped to the ground. "Thanks. Appreciate it," he said. "I'll be waiting to hear from you." He waved at the three of them and ambled to his car.

Everyone remained silent until his vehicle was three blocks away. Heather had gripped Dave's arm, her hold threatening his blood flow. "Easy, sweetheart. Easy," he said. "He's gone."

She breathed deeply. "You don't understand. I wasn't afraid of him, David. I really wasn't." Her voice shook, but she was adamant. "I wanted to kill him. That's all I thought about. Until I remembered what you said."

"What I said?"

"You said I can't fight a bullet."

MAYBE IT WAS HAVING a van again, or maybe it was the colorful Girlfriends sign on the sides, but a week later Heather and Tiffany were surrounded by kids each time they cruised the streets. Heather kept to her old route and word traveled fast, but clearly not to Brenda, the girl who'd gotten involved with the drug ring. Heather worried about her. Brenda hadn't reappeared anywhere since.

On her rounds Wednesday night, Heather had stopped at the Youth Center when two kids she'd picked up were running fevers and needed somewhere to go.

Julie Rogers, an excellent case manager, took them in. Her first question reinforced Heather's decision to create Girlfriends.

"When are you opening the new place? We need it. We're overflowing."

"That bad, huh? Sounds like we'll fill up the first week."

"I'm afraid so." The woman guided one of the ill youngsters to a chair. "Come on, hon. We'll get you to bed real quick."

Heather followed with the other feverish girl. "We're opening January first, holiday or not. So, if you have referrals the week before or so, call me and we'll set up the paperwork."

"Are you staffed?"

"Not fully," she replied. "I want the best, so…are you looking?" She'd grab Julie in a heartbeat if she was available.

The woman smiled but shook her head. "Thanks anyway. But I know someone. I trust her work, and I'd provide a reference."

"Good enough. Tell her to send me a résumé at Welcome Home." Heather turned to leave. "By the way, any sign of Brenda? The one who—"

"I remember," interrupted Julie, shaking her head. "Nothing. Sorry."

Too bad, thought Heather as she returned to her van. Brenda needed help, the kind of help Heather would be able to offer. The components of the Girlfriends project were falling into place like pieces in a jigsaw puzzle. Each part had its purpose. The people, the place, the program. And now with Mark Warner's contribution of an architect and experienced construction crew, the physical work was ahead of schedule. Dave's father remained the point man for the renovation, especially when she wasn't there.

Heather got behind the wheel again, and checked her rearview mirror. Yup. Patrick McCoy was there, too, tailing her as he did every time she went out. She'd given up protesting. As he'd said, "take it up with Dave. I'm following orders." Tonight, Anne was with him. A funny kind of date to have with an ex-husband.

"I can't let Dave bully me into this arrangement," she complained to Tiffany, "but I'd waste my breath arguing with him."

"What did you say?" asked Tiffany.

Heather tilted her head toward the back. "Him. Our tail. Now honestly, do you think we still really need someone watching over us?"

"Not with this brand-new baby we're driving." Tiffany hadn't hesitated. "On the other hand, I wouldn't go out alone, even with the new van."

"But…never mind." Sometimes the kids were alone out there, but she didn't have the heart to fight with everyone in her life. Dave was studying with his pals twice a week as well as on his own and working his regular shift. He still volunteered at Girlfriends on Saturdays. And afterward…after the work was done…well, he didn't want Saturdays with her to end.

Last weekend, he'd said, "Next week, Heather. Just us. No family. No scenes at country clubs. No work. Just you and me. Out together just like any other couple on a Saturday night."

With his gaze on her, and his fingers against her cheek, she'd had no desire to refuse. Normalcy. Wasn't that what she'd always wanted in her life?

So she'd agreed to this upcoming weekend. And every time she thought about an evening alone with David, her heart rate wasn't normal at all.

AN EVENING BY THEMSELVES? Not quite. Heather glanced around Minute Maid Park at the other forty thousand Houston Astros fans who filled the stadium. She grinned up at Dave after they found their seats. "I think you're afraid of being alone with me."

His eyes gleamed as he laughed. "No chance of that. I'm just giving you what you asked for. You wanted normal, and what could be more normal than baseball?"

"Nothing...except it's mid-October and this is a play-off game. The Astros are halfway to the World Series, and I don't even want to know how you got the tickets. Or how much you paid for them."

"Then don't ask."

"I just hope you didn't empty your bank account...."

Dave squeezed her hand. "My bank account is fine. Let's enjoy ourselves."

She had no argument with that. So far, she'd enjoyed every minute they'd spent together including the train ride on the light-rail system, which brought them right to the ballpark. It made sense to avoid the crush of the parking lot when the game let out later.

"This is my first time," she said slowly as she looked around the stadium, which featured a remarkable retractable roof, acres of real grass.

"In this ballpark?"

Minute Maid Park had recently replaced the Astrodome as the team's home stadium. She shook her head. "This is my first time at a professional baseball game."

He didn't say anything, and she poked him with her elbow. "Hey, did you think Dry Creek had a real baseball team?"

His hand covered hers, his thumb gently stroking her skin. "I didn't think about it at all. So, I'm very glad we're here. It's an extra-special night."

In truth, she didn't follow any sports team very much. Mark's big reaction to the news about where she was going clued her in about the play-offs and how big an achievement it was for the teams to get that far. She didn't realize Dave was such an ardent fan. How much did she really know about his likes and dislikes?

"So are you a baseball fanatic?" she asked.

"Fanatic? No, but I've always loved going to a game—especially with my dad. When you're inside a ballpark, you're in another world, and all the personal stuff is left outside the stadium. No matter what else was happening at home, everything was always fine at the ballpark."

"And after the game?"

He barked with laughter. "After the game, Dad would give me a ten-dollar bill, say that my mom didn't have to know about it, and then tell me to take care of her."

She wasn't surprised. Not with the way Patrick still looked at Anne.

"When I graduated college, I told him to take care of her himself if he was so concerned." He clasped her hand. "It shook him up, I'll tell you that."

"Sounds like a lot more than baseball happened in the ballpark."

He took a while before nodding. "Maybe so. Maybe my old man knew what he was doing. At least with me."

The players were being introduced over the state-of-the-art, 1400 speaker sound system, according to her program guide. The crowds cheered each man as he walked onto the field, but their loudest calls went to their favorites. A few minutes later, from her seat over the third base line, Heather heard the words "Play ball!"

By the end of the first inning, she was caught up in the action. Maybe because it was a play-off game. Maybe because Dave was having a great time coaching from his seat, and she enjoyed watching him. Maybe because she was part of something new and exciting and different. Heather felt wonderful.

"Now I know what you meant," she said when the teams were changing positions. She got to her feet and gestured around the ball field. “It really is another world in here.” She smiled up at Dave who immediately wrapped his arms around her and pulled her close. She hugged him back. So solid. So strong. She leaned into him, totally comfortable.

By the fifth inning, Heather knew if the Astros didn’t win, she’d be as disappointed as the rest of their fans. She knew enough about high school baseball to follow most of the action at a professional game. Dave filled her in on some technicalities around bites of their hot dogs.

“You’ve got some mustard…right there,” said Dave just before he licked the condiment from the corner of her mouth and lingered to steal a kiss.

“Cleanup detail?” she murmured.

“Anytime. Heather…? Maybe this…”

A blaring announcement from the speakers drowned anything Dave might have said. “Kiss Cam. Kiss Cam.” The announcement carried to every corner of the stadium.

“Wha…?”

Dave didn’t wait. His mouth was on hers before she completed the word, and he kissed her as though he were dying and needed air. As though she were his oxygen.

He pulled her to her feet, and she wrapped her arms around his neck, drawing him closer. Oh, God. She could get into this, with Dave. Only with Dave.

Suddenly, out of the corner of her eye, she saw herself and Dave—in full color—on a huge screen in Center Field. Forty thousand screaming fans saw them, too, shouting their encouragement. The ones nearby were clapping, catcalling, yelling for more.

Heather felt heat travel from her toes to her scalp in a nanosecond. What just happened? What part of baseball was a Kiss Cam?

But Dave was grinning. He looked…happy. Carefree. And so incredibly handsome.

"Your face!" he exclaimed. "It's priceless."

The people near them were still waving and applauding. So, Heather waved back. Dave did too, before reaching into his pocket.

"Cell phone," he explained as they sat down again.

"McCoy here. Yeah, Dad. I know. You saw everything, just like you were there. Gotta go." He glanced at Heather as he hung up and shrugged. "Dad. He was watching the game."

"Oh, my goodness. Who else…?"

He reached into his pocket again. "Yorkie. Yes, I'm with Heather. And no, she doesn't need protection from me, but you might!" He disconnected. "For crying out loud," he murmured. And the mobile vibrated again. "If it's Powers or Jazzman… Oh, Kathy. She's right here." He winked. "Your turn."

But it was Mark's voice she heard. "Are you okay, Heather? I'll talk to him if he's coming on too strong."

"No, no, Mark. I'm fine."

"Are you sure? That was some picture! Put McCoy on the line." She handed the phone over and shrugged. "He wants you."

After a moment Dave said, "Don't be an ass. I wouldn't hurt a hair on her head." Then Dave turned to Heather. "I'm shutting it off."

"Great idea."

"But you know that don't you?" His brow furrowed as he spoke. "What I said to Warner? I'd never hurt you." He stroked her cheek so gently that she raised her hand and pressed her palm to his.

She wanted to say, yes. That she trusted him with her life. With all her heart, she wanted to say, yes. But she couldn't. So, something was definitely wrong with her. Something that would prevent her from experiencing the happiness Kathy shared with Mark.

The crowd's attention was back on the field. "New

inning's starting," she said. But she let her hand remain in his and hoped he didn't realize she'd avoided his question.

CHAPTER TWELVE

PATIENCE. He simply needed more patience. Dave entered the Briefing Room almost a week after his baseball date with Heather, the woman constantly on his mind. He'd win her trust. In the end, he'd win. Until then, patience. He'd bet his career she already trusted him. Maybe she just didn't know it.

The truth was, he trusted her, too. Except when her judgment was clouded by her concern for the kids.

He went through his usual routine, glanced at the bulletin board, grabbed a chair and made small talk with his buddies. Yorkie hadn't shown up when the sergeant started roll call. Very unusual, and he hoped nothing was wrong.

Five minutes later, he had his answer. Eve would be out for a couple of days, and would probably be assigned to light duty when she returned. The sergeant looked at Dave. "You're on your own tonight. Powers, Jazzman—I want you to check in with him periodically. I'm working on a new schedule. McCoy, you'll have a partner in a day or two."

"Not necessary, sir. Wasn't Eve assigned to assist temporarily? Now that we've arrested the fourth perp, and the citizen is out of danger, I can handle it alone again."

"When I want your opinion, I'll ask." Dave wished he'd kept his mouth shut.

"Yes, sir."

"First announcement: reminder of the M.P. filed by one of our own. Officer Hank Landers's wife and two children have now been missing for four weeks and two days. And we've got nothing. People don't disappear into thin air."

Unless they want to. Dave looked around the room. A couple of glances were exchanged, a cough or two. Some cops stared at the ground. Did they have suspicions about Landers, or were they thinking about their own wives? Mac had a quick temper. Fielding drank too much. Those two were on their way to being Hank Landers clones. He hoped the department would step in before the worst happened. Maybe psychological and social services should be required to intervene at the first sign of a problem. Better yet, maybe a routine annual family session should be mandated.

At the end of the session, he made a note to call Eve the first chance he had. Her presence on his beat had eased his mind because of Heather. But that emergency was over. Now, he'd be back to his usual routines, which meant he couldn't cruise past Welcome Home as often as he'd like or past Girlfriends, either. At least, he'd put his dad on Heather's tail…no, today was Thursday, and Thursday wasn't an outreach night. Good. No worries there. He got into his assigned vehicle and began his patrol.

HEATHER STARED OUT her office window. She'd become such a daydreamer, she barely recognized herself. She couldn't stop thinking about Dave since the baseball game.

Everyone she knew had teased her about "the kiss" on the big screen, and it would have been hard to forget about Dave even if she'd wanted to. That kiss had been good, but their kisses…and more…later that night had been better. And left her wanting even more.

"Heath-er." Kathy's voice buzzed in the background. "It's Kathy calling Heath-er. Come in, Heather."

Heather swiveled in her chair and saw her sister in the doorway, her hands cupped around her mouth like a megaphone.

"You're in another world these days, kiddo. Something on your mind? Or is it some*one*?" asked Kathy with a knowing grin.

Heather felt her face burn, annoyed with her fair complexion. Embarrassment was so obvious.

Kathy laughed softly. "Oh. This is great."

"Go home, Kath." Heather motioned toward the exit. "I'm stopping at Girlfriends first."

Kathy shook her head. "Can't stay away even for a day, can you?"

"Thanks to Mark, everything's happening fast now, and I love to see the progress. The old appliances are out and at a secondhand store on consignment, and we're getting a professional six-burner stove for the redesigned kitchen."

Her sister waited a beat. "But *this* place won't be the same. I can't imagine Welcome Home without you."

"I'm not far away."

Kathy shook her head. "You know as well as I do that Girlfriends will take all your time, especially once the kids come."

Heather wouldn't insult her sister by denying it. "We have two interviews scheduled next week. We'll find someone to replace me."

"As if. There *is* no one else like you." Kathy

paused again, then continued with forced levity. "Now get ready for this... Guess who asked me about administrative positions here?"

"No clue."

"Anne McCoy."

"Dave's mom?" Heather was speechless for a moment. "What's up with that? She earns lots of money at that construction company. I don't get it."

"She said she wants something more. Different. A job working directly with people—where she feels she's making a difference."

"So, what did you tell her?"

"The truth. We have no openings here now. But I took her résumé anyway."

"I sure hope she doesn't ask me about Girlfriends. I'll need top-notch administrative help, but... Uh-uh."

Kathy was shaking her head. "She won't. She's too smart for that. Too smart to meddle with her son's happiness." Kathy seemed to be carefully choosing her words. "You do realize he's crazy about you, Heather. You're the only person in the room to him. And that's love, honey."

Without waiting for a reply, she turned on her heel and left.

"But, I'm afraid," Heather whispered, looking at the empty doorway.

She wanted the impossible. And no one could give it to her, not even her sister. There were no guarantees in life.

And then she started daydreaming about Dave again until she found herself parked at Girlfriends.

It was after five, and the construction team was getting ready to leave. One of the men gave her a quick walk-through, showing her where space had been opened up and new walls erected.

"But hold off on the painting," said the carpenter. "We're still working downstairs and the dust goes everywhere."

She'd postpone the volunteer painters, but maybe she'd contact Dave's mother about choosing colors. Anne seemed interested in that kind of stuff.

Dusk fell earlier at this time of year, and she let the men leave, with her thanks. The project was coming together. Her instincts were just fine in the work area of her life.

She locked the front door and walked toward her car just as another sedan rounded the corner, a single flashing light on top. Dave? It wasn't his usual vehicle.

She recognized Hank Landers instantly. In full

uniform this time, probably coming directly from work. She didn't have to wonder what he wanted. She took a deep breath and kept her eyes on him as he walked toward her.

The cop glanced toward the building. "This shelter is coming along. And when it's done, you'll have *two* places to hide people."

"That's right," she said quietly.

His mouth tightened in anger. "You're playing games with the wrong person, Ms. Marshall. I'm a bloodhound. I follow up until I get what I want."

Her thoughts raced. Landers had learned about Welcome Home. No doubt about that. He was as tall as Dave, but heavier. With her training, she could handle him. Except…he carried a gun. Would he use it? And where was Dave? He usually showed up when she needed him. Somehow he always knew.

But the street was quiet now, and she was on her own.

"What I want to know," said the cop, "is if my wife and kids are at your other place. Because, God damn it! I've been looking for over a month and this is my best lead!" His face had turned bright red and Heather could hear his raspy breathing.

She said nothing.

"I've got friends—friends on the force, even on the west side—who hate do-gooders like you. I know you're running the biggest safe house in the area. Now, are you going to take me to Mary Beth or do I have to tear the place down?" His low roar seemed to shake the live oaks. The man was losing whatever control he had when, in fact, he didn't know for sure his wife was at Welcome Home.

"Tearing the place down isn't necessary, Officer Landers," said Heather. "Come on, let's—"

"I knew you'd see reason," he interrupted, a victorious grin on his face. "Let's go to the shelter." He stepped toward his vehicle.

Heather chuckled as though the guy were amusing. "I was going to say, let's take a walk."

He reversed direction, his eyes conveying his excitement. She wanted to throw up.

She headed in the direction of her own car at a relaxed pace. He was ten feet behind her. "You're a lawman who thinks his wife ran to a shelter," she said, glancing at him over her shoulder. "You must be aware that ignoring a restraining order might jeopardize your job." She pitched her voice low, tried to sound as if she cared.

"Restraining order? How'd you know about that?" He cut the distance between them in half.

"Oh, come on, Hank. We see copies of them all the time. It's standard procedure, isn't it…in these situations?" And Mary Beth's copy was tucked safely in her plastic bag with all her other documents.

"Now that's where you're wrong," replied the cop. "Nothing's standard procedure with us. Do you think a little piece of paper like that means anything to me? I *am* the law. And I want my wife. And you're going to take me to her. Right now."

He grabbed her shoulder and spun her around. "Let go of me," she commanded in a low voice.

Surprisingly, he did. She searched in her purse for her car keys, pressed the remote and heard the locks open. "I can't take you to her," she said, "even if I wanted to. By now, she's probably safely in El Paso."

He stood there in shock, and Heather quickly opened her car door, slid behind the driver's seat and started the ignition.

"El Paso?"

"That's right," she called through the closed window. "Some women need more distance than others." El Paso was the farthest city from Houston she could think of.

She drove off, but her hands shook on the wheel. She lied only when she had to protect a life—or two or three. This time, if she included her own, the number rose to four.

THE NEXT AFTERNOON, Mary Beth stood in the dining room of Welcome Home surveying the women as they ate lunch, waiting for their reaction to the meal. She had suggested the menu, a combination of practicality and elegance. She'd scooped them out and stuffed the last of the tomatoes from the garden with a sauté of chopped ground meat, mushrooms and sweet onions, seasoned with a little of this and that. She'd mixed the whole concoction with rice, to stretch it, and topped each stuffed tomato with cheese and broiled it for a minute.

Several women looked her way and offered a thumbs-up. Her smile stretched from ear to ear. She'd always loved to cook, but she'd certainly never fed a crowd before. It was hard work, but creative and satisfying. Just like everything else she'd been doing at Welcome Home.

The group sessions, the individual counseling sessions and the practical you-need-to-support-yourself sessions consumed her days. She'd started to develop a résumé. Heather had promised to review her budget for job training. Maybe there'd be enough for Mary Beth to go to school and earn a culinary certificate. Even a basic one would give her an edge to apply for jobs in a restaurant. The hands-on experience she was getting at Welcome Home was an unexpected bonus.

She glanced over at her children with their new friends. Her kids ate what the adults ate, but Mary Beth had learned that most children weren't that adventurous. She always supplied a plate of PBJs at lunch.

Heather appeared in the doorway.

"Hungry?" asked Mary Beth. "Try one." She placed a stuffed tomato on a small plate.

"It not only looks wonderful, but smells wonderful, too," said Heather as she picked up a fork and tasted it.

She hoped Heather would like it. Didn't want her to have second thoughts about that job training.

"Mmm. This is delicious." Heather's eyes were closed as though she were savoring an exotic flavor. "You have provided the most excellent meals for us."

"With help," said Mary Beth quickly. She was only Stella's assistant. Stella was the professional, and Mary Beth wouldn't do anything without her approval.

"We need to talk about a few new things, so when

you're finished here, can you meet me in the lounge? Say, ten minutes?"

"Sure." Mary Beth watched Heather walk down the corridor, and a small knot formed in her stomach. New things required change. She didn't like change. Sometimes, not even changes for the better, which was stupid. *Change was part of growth.* Mary Beth had adopted that as her mantra when she was frightened. And she was frightened now.

Satisfied that everyone had been served, she said to Stella, "Heather's asked to speak with me. I'll be back as soon as I can."

Stella patted her shoulder. "You'll be fine. You're doing a great job."

Man, this place made her feel on top of the world. Sometimes she wished she could stay here forever. But even she realized that as good as it was, a shelter was not a permanent home for the children. Or for her. Ah, well. One day at a time is all she had to handle.

HEATHER WAS STANDING behind the couch waiting for her. Mary Beth saw the worry line on the counselor's forehead. The knot in her stomach became a lump. "What's wrong?"

"Come on. Let's sit down." Heather sat and patted the place next to her.

What choice did she have? Mary Beth sat and looked at Heather expectantly.

"I have good news and not-so-good news. And you'll have some decisions to make."

Mary Beth inhaled deeply. "Okay."

"First, the good news. We do have funding for you. You can attend the culinary program at the community college whenever you're ready. I just wanted you to know that you have that option."

Everything else went out of her head. "Thank you, thank you so much. I'll take any job while I go to school. And then try to find an upscale restaurant. This is great." At that moment, she saw a future for her and the kids.

"There's the other thing, Mary Beth."

Heather's tone of voice brought her back to reality. She gripped the arm of the sofa, and was shocked when Heather's hand clasped hers.

"I have some news, honey."

She nodded. This was not good. "Hank?"

"He's not giving up. He's made his way though every patrol division in the city and is now scouting the west side."

"The cops are going to help him, aren't they?" she managed to whisper.

"No. Not necessarily. We have a lot of excellent cops, too."

"All it takes is one...."

"Our security system is the best," Heather reassured her. "Even if he came to the front door, he couldn't get inside."

"Maybe." But if Hank ever showed up, he wouldn't think twice about shooting his way through.

"He won't do anything that drastic, Mary Beth, because he'd not only lose his job, he'd go to jail."

"But he's crazy, Heather. He won't think rationally. He'll just go after what he wants. Me. And the kids."

"I told him you were in El Paso."

Her head jerked up. "What? You've met him?"

Heather nodded. "Now you've got some thinking to do. Some choices to make. But you don't have to make them now. Take a breath. And another. Find your center."

She inhaled deeply, then exhaled. Inhaled again. Closed her eyes. Thought about green trees, open fields and a clear stream. Thought about her Megan and Neil running through the fields laughing. She opened her eyes.

"What kind of choices are you talking about?"

"If you'd feel safer, I can arrange for you to be transferred to a shelter in Dallas. That's a four-hour trip from here. We've worked with this shelter in the past. You won't lose anything in terms of training and planning a future."

Leave Welcome Home? After she'd become so comfortable here? "He keeps winning, doesn't he?"

"No, Mary Beth. He hasn't won. He won't win."

As empathetic as Heather was, she still didn't get it. "First, he forced me out of my house. Now he's forcing me out of my new home. He's still in control. And how can that be?" She couldn't hold back the tears. Didn't even try. "It's because he's got the connections," she sobbed. "Don't you see? A civilian can't do it. But a cop can."

She raised her head and stared at her counselor. "Don't marry him, Heather. That cop you're seeing. Don't do it."

"What? How did—"

"In a place like this, there are no secrets." Heather seemed so young, so innocent.

"Dave isn't like your husband."

"He will be. Even Hank was nice in the beginning. I actually—God help me—fell in love with him."

Heather started to get up from the couch. "Wait a minute," said Mary Beth. "What do you think I should do?"

"The choice is truly yours, Mary Beth. We're perfectly happy to have you stay. But if you don't feel safe here anymore, then we'd be perfectly happy to take you to Dallas. Unless he actually quits his job, or takes a leave of absence, he won't be able to nose around there like he's doing here."

"He's only got the nerve to do it because he's a cop," she whispered.

"That's not true. You've heard the others' stories. These guys are all about control, regardless of their careers."

But none of the others made the rounds of the domestic violence shelters. She scanned the familiar room. "I don't know. I just don't know."

"That's okay," said Heather, patting her arm. "Take some time and think about it."

"You do the same. Before it's too late."

IT WAS ALREADY TOO LATE. Heather thought about Dave constantly. Her feelings for him were as strong as they could be. She reminded herself of Kathy some months ago. Walking around in a daze with

Mark on her mind—and in almost every sentence she spoke.

But as deep as her feelings went now, she wasn't ready for commitment. Not unless Dave changed careers.

She'd left Mary Beth a few hours ago, and now she was ready to cruise the streets. Tiffany wasn't available that night, but if Dave's dad was outside ready to follow her, she'd go anyway. In fact, the only reason she didn't venture out alone was because she'd promised she wouldn't. That would have to be renegotiated.

She got the box of sandwiches and supplies from the kitchen and loaded the vehicle. When she drove out, Dave's mom and dad were waiting at the curb, Anne standing beside the car. She wore jeans, sneakers and an orange jersey. Clothes that a kid would wear. Heather waved and Anne walked over, opened the passenger door and got in.

"What are you doing?" asked Heather.

"I'm your partner tonight. Frankly, I've been wanting to do this for a while now."

CHAPTER THIRTEEN

SINCE WHEN HAD Anne McCoy wanted to ride the van? What was this all about? Kathy's words came back to her about Anne wanting a job that would make a difference. Oh, boy.

"Mrs. McCoy, I don't blame you for being bored back there." Heather pointed to Patrick's car, but Anne's raised eyebrows made Heather realize how that had sounded. She didn't mean Anne would be bored with Patrick, just with riding around two or three times a week. She apologized.

Anne chuckled and patted Heather's leg. "Oh, I know what you meant. Believe me, Patrick and I are definitely not bored."

Heather wasn't going to touch that, and didn't have to as her cell phone rang. She reached for it in the center console. "It's Dave."

Anne smiled, nodded.

"Hey," said Heather into the phone. "Your mom's sitting up here with me."

"Which means you're short staffed. But that's fine as long as Dad's following you."

"McCoy, we have to renegotiate this deal now that I have a reliable vehicle."

"And that would be negative."

"If that's cop talk, I don't like it."

"You just like to get your own way."

She glanced at Dave's mother. Anne's expression was carefully bland. "I need to get going—"

"Hang on a sec. I should have touched base with you last night when I found out my schedule's changed. I'm on my own again—on the beat. Eve's been pulled off. She's having a little trouble with the pregnancy."

"Oh, dear. I'm sorry to hear that. And that explains why I didn't see you yesterday when Landers came around Girlfriends after work." She laughed softly. "You've always managed to show up at the right time in the past."

"Landers? You should have called me. Heather, don't trust him if he shows up again. Not for a second. Speed dial my cell. Call 911. Do not find yourself alone with him."

She started to make soothing noises, but he cut her

off. "Staying out of trouble in the first place might help. You could keep a whole division busy all by yourself."

The last remarks weren't fair. If he weren't voicing such concern for her, she would have disconnected the call. "I've handled Landers twice. I can do it again. Nobody can watch me 24/7. So relax. I've got work to do. Goodbye."

She kept her eyes forward and started the van.

"It's beginning already." Anne sighed. "I knew it."

"Hmm."

"I love my son dearly. But if he doesn't change careers…" Anne tsked and muttered, "Oh, dear. I see a lot of wasted, empty years ahead."

"Hmm."

"A lot of heartache."

"And I see three kids near the park entrance, Mrs. McCoy."

"But you two really make such a good couple…."

Heather pulled up to the curb. She cut the engine. The kids were young. Really young. Maybe twelve or thirteen.

"Hey, guys. I'm Heather."

Two girls and a boy. They eyed her with suspicion.

"Hungry?"

Of course they were. She turned toward Anne. “Could you get the box of…?”

She didn’t have to finish the question. Anne came toward her with sandwiches, drinks and blankets. “I thought they could use these, too. The evenings are getting cool.”

The woman’s logic was fine, but her blinking eyelids told their own story. Anne’s heart had taken over. She’d have to learn to control her emotions and set personal boundaries to be effective. Establishing those boundaries always proved to be the hardest thing a caseworker had to learn.

“So’s how’s park living?” asked Heather as the kids scoffed their food.

“It’s okay,” said the boy.

“We made, like, a little apartment under one of the giant turtles they have,” said a girl, pointing to a round cement structure. The other two smiled and nodded. “That’s our place. It’s really cool.”

So they thought all their problems were solved. “Anybody hurting?” asked Heather. “Sick? Need any supplies?”

She pulled out her mobile. “I’m glad you’ve got a place, but here’s what I do every time we visit.” She went into her “call home” and Youth Center speech.

No takers. Maybe next time. At which point she'd try to have a private talk with each of them. "I'll be back Monday night," she said. "Take care of yourselves." She established eye contact with each of them. "And if you need help, ask somebody—anybody—to call me or the Youth Shelter. They'll take you in day or night." She gave each youngster a business card.

She motioned to Anne, and they returned to the vehicle.

"I hate leaving them out there," said Anne.

"I know. But they're not ready to come in yet."

Anne seemed lost in thought and didn't reply immediately. "One African-American, one Hispanic, one white. A microcosm of the city."

"That's common with young runaways. They don't have to prove themselves to a gang. Their issues don't involve turf wars. They're simply—if you can use that word—running away from a bad home."

"Or what they *think* is a bad home."

Heather had to agree. Kids that ran away overnight to a friend's house were included in the researchers' statistics, too. But these kids had gone further than that.

She glanced into her rearview mirror. Patrick kept a steady pace. Funny, she'd almost forgotten he was there. Come to think of it, she'd bet money the kids didn't notice him, either.

"Your husband is really good," said Heather.

"Ex. You mean ex-husband."

Heather grinned. "It's kinda hard to remember that."

"Oh, hush," said Anne, making a production of searching her pocketbook for a pen and paper. "I have an idea. Let's buy some prepaid phone cards to give out. Then they won't have to ask a stranger for help."

"I'll put it on the wish list," said Heather. "It's a great thought."

She pulled onto the service road and cruised the right lane. Her skin began to tingle as she approached the run-down strip mall where the incident had happened. Some incident. Knives and her. And what seemed like the whole police department. Tonight, she counted about six or seven youths in the parking lot.

For a moment, she got lost in déjà vu. Her heart raced, she gripped the wheel. Only perps were known to go back to the scene of the crime. Victims rarely wanted to.

"What's wrong, Heather?"

"Nothing. I'm fine." She took a deep breath, yanked the wheel and parked in her old spot. Patrick drove past the entrance. Probably didn't want to appear too obvious, but Heather gulped as he disappeared down the road.

Heather opened her door, walked around the front of the van and stopped dead. "Brenda! Oh, my God. What happened to you?"

Tears began streaming from the girl's eyes. One of her cheeks was so swollen, the eye above was almost closed. Her bruises showed black upon her brown skin. Heather ran to her, arms extended, and held her.

"Oh, sweetie. Who did this?"

But the teen was crying too hard for Heather to understand her.

"Let's see if we can help her," said Anne in a soothing voice. She held a plastic bag of ice and some paper towels. "I took the cubes from the cooler."

"Thanks." Heather placed the ice pack carefully on Brenda's cheek. The girl barely flinched.

"You need a little barrier," said Anne, as she inserted the paper towels between the ice pack and Brenda's skin. "We don't want ice burn."

"Thanks again."

"So what happened, Brenda?" asked Heather once more ignoring the audience.

"I—I went home…" came her garbled reply. "But… but…"

Heather heard Anne gasp. "I'm so sorry, Brenda. Sometimes home is just not the best place to be. Sometimes it can even be the worst place."

"Yeah, I knew that…but I was hoping…and I was tired."

Heather could see the change in her. She had once been a spirited and yes, defiant, child. Now, she hit bottom. She needed to understand that bottom didn't mean the end.

"There are people in this world who want to help you, Brenda," said Heather. "But you have to give them a chance."

"Like you?"

"That's right. And like Julie at the Youth Center."

Brenda nodded and winced. "Miss Julie was all right."

An understatement. "Do you want to go to the center again? It's your decision."

Heather reached for her cell phone and offered it to Brenda. Brenda's fingers wrapped around it and she punched in the number to the Youth Center. The kid had learned it by heart, but Heather wasn't surprised. A sharp memory served as a survival skill.

Silence seemed to hang in the air as Brenda, in a shaking voice, asked to speak to Julie.

When a car pulled into the lot and drove slowly past them to the main parking area, Heather wasn't surprised to seee Patrick behind the wheel. He and his nondescript car blended into the environment perfectly. Goodness, tonight was a big success. So far, Heather had no complaints.

An hour later, Heather and Anne were on their way to Welcome Home. Julie had picked up Brenda and a second girl. The other youngsters had melted away before Julie's arrival but knew when the van would come around again. Anne had been quiet on the ride back so far.

"Was this a typical night for you?" she asked.

Heather thought for a moment. "In some ways, it was better."

"Because of Brenda?"

"Yes. It's hard to measure long-term success, but now I have some hope for her. Real hope."

"I just wanted to cuddle her and take her home with me."

"I know," Heather said.

"Am I that obvious?"

Heather grinned. "You've got nothing to hide. Being a good mom is a special gift, and tonight you gave the kids a dose of Anne McCoy mothering.

They need that just like they need a plan and goals and reassurance to go along with a secure home."

Heather parked the van in the Welcome Home lot, and she and Anne walked to the front of the building. Patrick strode toward them.

"You're just in time, Pat," Anne said. "And by the way, you did a great tailing job tonight. I hardly remembered you were there."

"I'm not sure that's a compliment," said the retired cop, but he winked at Heather.

Heather giggled. "Oh, it is," she said. "Even I forgot you were there except when you drove past the strip mall."

"Were you concerned?"

Heather looked away for a moment. "For a second, yeah. But only for a second." And then she had been fine—almost like her old self. "Anne did a great job tonight, too." Heather covered a yawn. "For a rookie."

"But I don't want to stay a rookie," said Anne in a voice that brooked no question. "Heather, what do I have to do to start a second career in your field?"

"What?" interrupted Patrick, his voice rising with surprise. "I'm retired, and you're going to start over?"

Anne spun in a circle, arms out to the night sky.

"You bet I am. I'm only fifty years old, Patrick. I have time for a second act!"

She stopped in front of the man, her face tilted up toward his. "Are you with me on this?" She raised her index finger. "Before you answer—I warn you—"

"I don't need any warnings, woman. If you're happy and excited, I might even join you for an encore." He put his hands around her waist and twirled her in the air as though she weighed nothing.

Heather disappeared before they could notice her. And for the first time since they'd left Houston, images of George and Jolene filtered through her mind. She hoped they were doing well.

MARK'S CAR WAS PARKED in the street when Heather finally got home. She was glad of the company to help her wind down.

But Kathy and Mark didn't look very happy when Heather stepped into the kitchen. "We're so glad you're home."

"So am I. What's up?"

Kathy glanced at her fiancé, then at Heather. "Pour yourself a cup of coffee first. Have some Mississippi Mud Pie."

Her evening had been full enough. She was more

than willing to postpone whatever they wanted to share. "Mississippi Mud Pie. My favorite! Forget the coffee. This cake requires a side of milk." Heather opened the fridge and poured a glass, then gestured at the dessert. "What's the occasion?"

"My mom," said Mark, shrugging. He started to pace.

"Your mom? That's the explanation?"

"She's trying to be nice." Kathy raised a brow at Heather. "If she's any nicer, I won't fit into my wedding dress. But this cake was for you."

Mark spoke up. "She says it's an apology."

"I don't need an apology."

Kathy took the carafe and refilled Mark's cup. "Believe me, I've received a mountain of apologies since the night at the country club. It's enough."

Heather dug into the cake.

She looked up. "Okay. Spill it. What's really going on?"

"Hank Landers called here tonight," replied Kathy.

Heather forgot to chew.

"He strongly suggested that I keep you in line. Guess he found out that I was the executive director and that you actually work for me." Kathy shrugged. "Like it matters."

"Get to the point, honey." Mark jumped impatiently into the conversation. "He's on a rampage looking for his wife and kids. I don't like this. Not at all. I've never heard of personal contact between the abuser and the shelters. But what the hell do I know about social work anyway?"

Things were coming at her too fast. "This is extremely unusual, so start from the beginning," said Heather. "What else did he say?"

"He wanted me to confirm that his wife was in El Paso," said Kathy.

"Which you didn't."

"Of course not. I told him I knew nothing at all about his wife and hung up."

"Then he called again," Mark said.

"At which time I repeated myself and said that even if I did know his wife, I wouldn't tell him a thing. And please don't call back."

"And that's when the man blew up," said Mark, "and I got on the phone. That's when he slammed the receiver. But at least there haven't been any more calls… Pack some clothes, Heather. You and Kathy are coming to my place tonight."

He sounded just like Dave. She swallowed her protest. She even managed a tiny smile. "Okay. But first we're stopping at the police station. I'm filing a restraining order against John Henry Landers."

He nodded. "I like that idea."

"I also want to call Dave," she said in a quiet voice.

"Really?" said Kathy. "Think he'd care?"

"I think he'd go bonkers if I didn't."

She punched his cell number, but got no answer. That meant he'd probably responded to a call from his dispatcher and was out doing his job.

FLOODLIGHTS ILLUMINATED the police station and the front parking area. Heather got out of the backseat as soon as Mark stopped the car. "This shouldn't take too long."

"Slow down," said Kathy. "We're going with you."

Who knew the place would be so busy at night? Heather looked around as she walked through the front door to the Information Desk. "I want to report a stalker."

The officer picked up a phone and spoke into it. A minute later another police officer appeared from inside the main working area. "This is Officer MacDonald."

The cop grunted and motioned her to follow. When Kathy and Mark started walking, too, the man turned, his brows drawn.

"We're family," said Mark.

"Family can wait here." Heather darted a glance at her sister and Mark and shrugged. Then she followed the cop.

"So, who's stalking you? A husband? A boyfriend?" asked the officer after he sank into his seat. He reached into a drawer and pulled out some forms.

"Definitely not." Heather sat at the edge of her chair.

Maybe it was the tone of her voice, but that got the cop's attention. And she wasn't sure she wanted it. His eyes appraised her from head to foot. "There's always a boyfriend when there's a restraining order," he muttered.

He looked at the paper on his desk. "Name?"

Heather stood up. "Never mind. I'll handle it myself."

"Whatever you want." The cop sat back in his seat and folded his hands across his stomach.

Heather took several steps toward the exit when she heard her name and saw Jazzman. "Hey, Jazz."

"Looking for Dave?" he asked, falling in step with her.

"It would be great if he were here, but I didn't expect him." She inclined her head toward the guy she'd just left. "What's his problem?"

"Mac? He's an ass."

Heather started to laugh. "I'm glad I didn't cause his attitude. What a creep."

"We can't all be as perfect as McCoy and yours truly," he said with an irreverent grin. "So how can I help you?" He waved her into a chair and sat behind a desk.

She paused. Jazz was a great guy. He'd come to her aid in the parking lot, a devoted cop. But still, she paused. At this point, Landers's grudge targeted her. If Mary Beth were truly in danger, she wouldn't have hesitated. But Mary Beth couldn't be safer unless she really were in El Paso. And Heather was used to taking care of herself. She'd tell Dave about the phone calls tomorrow. "It was great seeing you Jazz," she said, rising to her feet. "Take care of yourself."

Before she could leave, a tall man in uniform motioned to Dave's friend. "Come with me. We've got a DV situation out there."

"Sure, Captain."

Heather understood. Domestic Violence. The kind of call cops dreaded most. Emotions ran hottest in these situations. No telling what weapons might be stashed in the house.

"McCoy needs a negotiator."

She grabbed Jazzman's sleeve. "Dave? Where?"

"Who's she?" asked the captain.

"McCoy's girlfriend."

"The woman who was almost killed by that drug runner?" The man studied her for a moment. "We'll call you when it's over."

Not good enough. She ran to the entrance area. "Mark, we're following that police car. Dave's in trouble."

THE MAN ON THE OTHER SIDE of the door had a gun and he was promising to use it on himself, his wife and two children. Dave had sent Powers to explore other possible access to the first-floor apartment.

Nothing is ever routine on the job.

On the plus side, Dave had established a dialogue with the man before he drew the gun. On the minus side, they were still separated by a door and walls. He'd keep on talking until a negotiator specialist showed up.

"Hey, Robert," Dave ventured. "I know you don't really want to hurt your wife or your kids. Tell me what you want, man. Just talk to me." The guy had lost his job. The neighbors had told him.

A marked car pulled up quietly. Jazz and the captain. He waved them over.

"I'm better off dead," came the voice inside the apartment.

"You don't really believe that, Robert," called Dave. "I know you lost your job. But we've got people who can help you find one."

"I can't feed my kids. I can't pay the rent. I'm hungry! What kind of a man am I?"

"We can help you, Robert. We help people get jobs all the time. My pal, Jazzman, is the man who can help you out. Help you get what you need. He's right here with me."

Silence.

Dave checked his watch. "I've been at it for thirty-five minutes," he said to the others. "And Powers says there's no other way in." He glanced to where Powers had established a perimeter. Too many nosy neighbors were hanging around. Powers needed help.

"I know about lots of jobs," Jazz called. "But what kind do you want?"

"My kids are hungry."

"We can do that, Robert," said Jazz. "I'll get hamburgers for everybody. For you, too. And you'll feel better. And then you're going to do something for me."

They didn't like silence.

"Robert! Are you listening? You gotta keep talking to me, man, so we know you're okay."

"I'm not okay. I'm better off dead. We're all better off dead."

"You know that's not true, Robert," said Jazzman in a voice as smooth as his name. "So, let's talk about the job you really want."

Dave listened with half an ear as Jazzman continued communicating with the man. He was working the crowd now, forcing room for the ambulance he'd called. No sirens. No flashing lights.

Then he glanced up…and saw her. Illuminated by the moonlight, Heather was more beautiful to him than ever. She stood quietly, as immobile as a still-life painting, simply watching him. With eyes filled with love.

"Go home, sweetheart." His voice cracked. "Please."

She extended her hand to him. "Give me your keys. I'll be waiting."

He complied without another word. Kathy and Mark were there, and he knew Heather must have talked them into this madness, but he didn't understand why or how. He just wanted them gone from the scene.

Heather smiled at him, and they left. Relieved, he

redoubled his efforts to push the growing crowd farther back. That's when he noticed the local television cameras. The reporters had picked up the call on their police scanners, and now they had a story.

CHAPTER FOURTEEN

HEATHER DOZED on the couch with the television on, coming awake when the story was featured on the local news channel. She watched Dave doing his job, heard him interviewed by the reporters, but couldn't see or hear what Jazzman was doing, which in her opinion was appropriate. The reporters stayed next to the perimeter, which made Dave one of the more easily accessible officials.

He'd been the first on the scene about the same time Heather had been at the police station, and now it was nearing 2:00 a.m. The cable news continued to keep her company while she fought to stay awake. But it was a losing battle.

A sharp rap on the door woke her. She jumped to her feet, dizzy for a moment, then remembered where she was and ran to open it.

"Welcome home." She took him by his arm and urged him inside, then kicked the door shut.

"Everything turned out fine," he said, exhausted but smiling. "Robert is in the psych unit at the hospital, counselors are with the wife and kids. They'll qualify for services. And Jazz is still with the HPD shrink…I promised to call in the morning."

"Why'd he let you leave?"

"Because I said someone special was waiting for me at home." He leaned back to look at her. "So, why are you here?" he asked gently.

Why was she here? She winced. Had he no clue about how she felt about him? She wouldn't allow the hurt to show and somehow managed to produce a smile. "I'm your backup, McCoy. Finally, *I'm* helping *you.*"

"You can't admit it, can you?" he asked, his voice still soft.

She understood what he was asking. Her mouth opened to tell him…but nothing came out.

"I'm so crazy in love with you, Heather, that you're part of who I am. So, if I have to wait a little longer, I will. And one day, I'll hear the words from your beautiful sexy mouth."

Tears pooled in her eyes and ran down her face. Dave tried to brush them away. "Aw, Heather. Don't cry over me."

Her heart swelled to bursting. She pulled him

toward the back of the apartment. “Dave…I want to hold you. And show you…”

“Sweetheart, I know how you feel. You don’t have to prove…”

She stopped and cupped his face with her hands. “Sometimes, honor is overrated…. We could…”

A grin crossed his face. “You think?”

“Only with you, Dave. Only with you.”

He gathered her against him, locking her in his grip so tightly she couldn’t breathe for a moment. And then his mouth covered hers, and her thoughts dissolved to nothing.

She kissed him freely. And felt his clear response against her body.

“I need a shower,” he murmured.

He didn’t seem to want to leave her even for a minute. “Want company?”

“Only if it’s you.”

“Oh, it’ll be me all right.” She reached for the top button of his shirt, slid it through the hole, then kissed his bare skin beneath. He stopped breathing.

“You’re going to kill me, Heath….”

“Yeah…I know….” And she opened the second button. Then the third, sprinkling kisses, licking his skin and feeling him shiver.

"Hang on, sweetheart. I've got to get rid of this." He unstrapped his gun belt and disappeared for a moment. Heather stood in the hallway, stunned. She'd forgotten all about that part of his uniform. Maybe that was a good sign.

He was back in a jiffy, shirt gone. "Now where were we?" he asked as he began to kiss her again. "I think two can play this game." He nibbled his way down her neck to the V of her shirt. One button open. Two buttons open. He nuzzled the cleft between her breasts, made his way over her bra. She felt his warm breath through the thin material, arousing her, sending shivers down to her toes. Her legs felt weak. She held on to him.

"I swear to God," gasped Dave, "this time it's going to take longer."

But his arousal was evident, and she was as ready as he. "I don't think so," she gasped.

A short time later, however, as the hot water flowed over them, Dave took his time moving the sudsy washcloth from her neck to her toes. Along her spine, across her bottom. Along the outside of her leg, then inside, traveling to her inner thigh, and higher. He brushed lightly against her most sensitive spot. She had to grab his shoulders for balance.

"I love every part of you," he whispered. "You're beautiful, Heather. And I love how you respond to me. Sweet…sweet…let's keep going…." But his hand remained there, pulsing against her until she was caught in his rhythm. "Oh…oh…." Short breaths. Little air.

He only stopped stroking when her entire body screamed for release…again.

She glanced up at him. "I'm taking charge now. It's only fair."

"Whatever you want…" She smiled, touched him and heard him catch his breath. Her fingers traveled lightly up and down his erection.

"Heath-er." His voice shook. "Slow down…slower…"

She looked up at his taut face, full lips, eyes as dark as night. His hands pressed against the sides of the shower stall to keep his balance. "I'm ready, too," she whispered, fumbling in the soap dish for the condom.

Despite his need, he entered her with care, nudging her against the shower wall, fitting himself to her, allowing her to absorb him. And then she arched forward, holding on to his shoulders, knowing she was safe. He scooped her up, and she wrapped her legs around his hips. She caught his rhythm in two strokes and then they moved as one.

They finally collapsed to the floor, drowning in a flood of pleasure. Exhausted.

"You're amazing," he gasped. "There's no one in the world like you."

"Or you."

He shut the spigot with his toes, and she stared at him. "I never knew how wonderful a shower could be." Her genuine surprise provoked giggles from her, but Dave's laughter rang deeper. To Heather, he looked as young as a boy. No lines. No furrows. Full of innocent delight.

He helped her up. Ran kisses all over her neck. "The best is yet to come," he whispered. "All you need to do is trust me."

"I'm working on it. Almost there." Her brain had just about caught up to her heart.

DAVE AND HEATHER arrived at Girlfriends at noon, later than they'd planned. But Patrick and Anne had covered the details with the other volunteers.

"Sure you're all right, son?" The elder McCoy walked quickly toward Dave. "You had quite an evening."

His dad didn't know the half of it. "Me? You're the one who should still be sleeping. Why'd you hang around so long last night?"

Patrick glared at him through tired eyes slightly bloodshot, then turned toward his ex-wife. "He still doesn't get it. Smart as a whip and still doesn't get it."

Of course he got it. "I'm your son. I love you, and you love me. That's fine. But I'm a cop, and I do my job." And why the hell were they having this conversation anyway? Especially in front of Heather who still harbored doubt.

"And I'm a father, and I do my job, too."

"Shush, Patrick," said Anne. "He looks fine. Better than ever." She studied her son. "Did you debrief yet?"

"Last night, and again this morning on the phone. My head's on straight. Enough?"

Anne nodded, then kissed him. "Until the next time."

Dave glanced uneasily at Heather who was absorbing the conversation. He might as well be up-front. "There's always a next time. You understand that?"

"What do you think?"

He nodded but said nothing. She understood the job all right, but her fears were not the same as his mother's. She trusted his instincts and his knowledge, but Heather still didn't trust cops. To her, the phrase "true-blue" was not reassuring. These two women in his life were not coming from the same place at all.

"I think we have work to do here," he said to Heather. "Let my folks go home."

"Of course!" Heather exclaimed. "And thank you so much." She turned to Anne. "Can you think about colors for the bedrooms upstairs and how to decorate them?"

"Consider it done. And by the way, I'd like some of that career advice I'd mentioned. When can we speak?"

"Mom, you're putting her on the spot."

Anne waved away his concerns. "It's just informal."

"How about over lunch on Monday?" suggested Heather.

Dave searched her face but found nothing but friendly interest. "Don't let my stubborn mother bulldoze you into anything you don't want to do."

"And how often does that happen?" Heather asked quietly.

He felt his body stir. She'd come to him of her own volition. A precious gift. He looked from one woman to the other, then glanced at his dad. "What is it with our attraction to strong women?"

"That's easy," Patrick said, his voice not easy at all. "They keep life interesting. And keep us grounded. And when they choose us...well, we're the lucky ones. It took me half a lifetime to discover that they're our salvation."

"Want to tell them now?" he asked Anne softly.

His folks didn't have to say a word. Dave knew what would come next. "When am I walking you down the aisle, Mom?"

THE REST OF THE WEEKEND passed by in a rush, and Monday morning seemed to arrive far too quickly. A mystery to Heather, who was now in her office, wearing her administrator and counselor hats. It was already November. Kathy's wedding loomed only a month away, and Girlfriends would open shortly after that.

Her phone rang. Lisa Connors. She'd moved to town permanently, staying with Eve and Larry until further notice. Eve seemed much stronger now, but she needed to keep her feet up as much as possible. "Frankly," Lisa said, "it's Larry who really wants me around. He's more nervous than Eve."

"Maybe you'll stop him from driving her crazy."

"I sure hope so. And now that I'm a new Houstonian, I'm so excited to find out all about Girlfriends."

"Just what I wanted to hear." They set a date for the next day.

Just as Heather hung up, the phone rang again.

"Heather? This is Mary Beth. Can we talk now?"

"Sure. In five minutes in the lounge." Phone calls to job applicants would have to wait. Mary Beth took priority.

As soon as she saw her, Heather knew the other woman had made her decision.

"I'll need to leave here someday," said Mary Beth. "So it might as well be now."

Heather studied the pacing woman who was trying so hard to be brave. "O-kay," she drawled. "We can certainly make arrangements for you. Tell me how you arrived at this decision."

Mary Beth nodded. "In the end, it was rather easy. How can I walk the streets of Houston safely? How can I enroll in the culinary training here? I know my husband, Heather. He won't respect any restraining order. As soon as I try to make a new life, he'll find me. He'll find the kids." She braced her hands against the back of the couch and leaned forward, head down. "No. I can't take that chance."

"Dallas?"

To her surprise, Mary Beth shook her head. "I'd

rather go out of state. He's got too many buddies in Texas." Then the tears came. "My…my parents don't know where I am. They must be worried. Who knows what Hank told them?"

And why hadn't these parents helped their daughter? But Heather didn't ask. She knew the answer. They didn't realize what was happening. Hank had probably spun a complex web of lies and rationalization. Some abusers managed to fool the world for years.

"I'll try to arrange something for tonight," said Heather, options racing through her mind. "We've got connections everywhere. But it might mean a change of climate."

"Then my kids will learn about the four seasons firsthand." The woman was resolute. "I'll start packing."

"You won't lose your access to training, Mary Beth," said Heather. "I promise you that."

"I'm counting on it." The woman left to tell her children.

"If you need backup," called Heather, "I'm here." Speaking with Megan and Neil was going to be harder than making the decision to leave.

An hour later, Heather came into Kathy's office.

"I'm escorting the Landers family to Minneapolis tonight—an 8:30 flight. I'll be back tomorrow afternoon. Gene is driving us to the airport at six in his car. If we arrive too early, we'll circle the airport until it's time to go. Can you make the rounds tonight? Tiffany will go with you, and the kids are expecting us."

"Yes, I can. And I'll give Gene Friday off. He's been putting in a lot of time."

Heather waited for her sister to absorb the real meat of the conversation. It took only a few seconds. "All right," said Kathy. "Minneapolis is fine...if that's what Mary Beth wants."

"I agreed with her decision, Kath. In her circumstances, she'll never feel free in Houston."

Kathy stared at her. "I'll keep my cell phone on, so check in with me every fifteen minutes until you're all on that plane. I want to monitor this transfer. You hear me?"

"Yes, ma'am." Heather gave her sister a mock salute. "Take it easy. Don't we always keep in touch?"

"Oh, Lord," Kathy said, "every time we go through this, I'm a nervous wreck. And I feel like we've lost a friend."

"I don't. I think of it as saving lives."

"But on a personal level, I wish Mary Beth could just have a safe life right here. I wish we could…I don't know…"

"Fix the world?"

"Yes."

"We're doing it, Kath, the way we always do it. One person, then another and another…"

Kathy started to smile. "I guess that's why it takes so darn long."

Heather nodded and left the room. She had more work to do, and she needed to call Dave. No point in him passing by the building in the hopes of seeing her that evening.

HANK LANDERS FINISHED his shift on Monday afternoon and drove away from his station house. Maybe Mary Beth really was in El Paso. Or hiding in a quiet safe house apartment, which could be anywhere. Or maybe she was in a motel. The damned city had so many motels, he couldn't count 'em. All Hank knew was he hadn't found Mary Beth anywhere yet.

Shit! He'd spent the whole friggin' weekend investigating for nothing. The whole damned weekend. He didn't need that idiot wife anymore. But the kids. They were his.

There was only one more shelter in the city he hadn't personally visited. Not that he'd gotten into any of them. But he had connections. His buddies had helped him out. He knew how it worked. A favor for a favor. A person never knew what the future held. *Welcome Home.* What a stupid name. The whores who lived there deserved all the misery they could find.

IN HER OFFICE at five forty-five that evening, Heather checked her pocketbook for the computer-issued airline tickets and driver's license for identification at the airport. She'd retrieved a few personal items from home earlier, which she'd placed in an ordinary tote bag to carry on the plane.

Kathy stood in her doorway.

"Are you and Tiff set to go now?" Heather asked.

"We are. Just stopping by to wish you luck. Don't be concerned about the street kids. We'll be out there tonight."

"Thanks, Kathy. Dave's parents will be trailing you. You'll be fine." She shrugged. "I can't get them to stop yet."

A satisfied expression settled on Kathy's face. "They can continue as long as they want with no complaints from me. Now tell me about the Landers family. How are Mary Beth and the kids?"

"Neil's angry. Megan doesn't understand. But Mary Beth is pretty calm. She keeps telling them that the important thing is that they're all together. And that they can make a home anywhere as long as they're together."

"Smart to focus on simple truths. No grandiose schemes and big promises."

"Mary Beth is a sensible woman. She just needs a fair chance. I'm meeting them and Gene at the back entrance in just a bit."

Kathy nodded and was gone. Five minutes later, Heather was about to leave her office, when her intercom buzzed. She glanced at the readout. Diana was probably checking on her. She picked up the receiver.

"There's a uniformed officer here," the guard said immediately. "Said he was sent on a 911 call, so I let him in. Now he's asking for a Mrs. Landers. And I said we don't have anyone by that name."

"Are you on speakerphone?" asked Heather.

"No."

"Good. You said the right thing. I'll be there in a minute."

"I'll tell him that."

Heather called Gene's cell phone. "Change of plans. Get the Landers family back to their suite and tell Mary Beth to lock the door. I want every resident in lockdown until further notice. Then wait to hear from me. Pass the word to the staff."

She hurried out of her office, her footsteps echoing as she went to the reception area. She opened the solid metal door separating the front area from the back and pulled it shut behind her. And there stood Hank Landers, big, bulky and looking very official in his blues.

"I know she's here. Now, bring her out with the kids."

Heather met his angry gaze. She braced herself and quietly said, "El Paso."

"Bullshit!" The word exploded, released on a breath reeking of alcohol. She saw his lips thin and his fingers curl into fists as huge as George's. She blinked.

"Mary Beth's got to be here," the cop continued. "She's nowhere else. I've checked. And besides, she's too chicken to go far away."

Heather forced a casual shrug. "Lots of our clients go elsewhere, Officer Landers. That's the truth. If you doubt it, that's your problem, not mine."

"I don't believe a word you're saying," he said,

moving toward her. "So we're going to take a walk back there and see."

She stared at him, but aimed her words at Diana. "Step on it, please."

"Yes, ma'am."

"Go ahead," laughed the cop. "Use your alarm system. Get the cops here. Whose side do you think they'll take?"

Heather's brain stopped working. For a moment. She wanted to believe—had no choice but to believe—her cops would do the right thing.

With his triumphant smile still in place, Landers took another step toward her. "The hell with both of you! I'm going inside."

Could she take him down? Heather's mind raced with alternatives as she stood squarely in front of the door. "It's locked tight," she said in a calm voice. "Can only be opened electronically." And she would never give the order.

"No problem." He reached for his gun.

You can't fight a bullet. She coughed to distract him. "You don't really want to do that," she said quietly.

He glared at her. "No woman tells me what to do."

Buy time. Keep talking. "I wouldn't think of telling you anything, Officer Landers. I'm simply asking—"

She never finished the sentence. His left hand knocked her sideways as though she were a toy. She hadn't seen it coming despite all her training. She stumbled and hit the wall. Then, he drew his gun. She managed to regain her balance….

"She can't hide from me!" the cop roared, firing two rounds at the door latch.

The man was crazy. Certifiable. She had no weapon to match his gun. Where was Dave? Where was Powers? Or Jazzman?

"Drop it!" She had her answer.

She remained against the wall, her cheek throbbing. But Landers spun around and smiled at Dave. "It's okay, buddy. You remember me. I'm HPD. We're family."

She wanted to vomit. Family. A cop like Hank could never, ever be part of hers. But which family would Dave choose?

"Drop it nice and easy," said Dave, his gun pointing at the other cop.

She had her second answer.

No one moved. Two cops. Two guns. Two women.

"Put it down, Landers," repeated Dave, "and we'll talk all about it outside. Maybe salvage your sorry-ass career."

Heather said nothing. Landers looked down at his gun, looked around the room, then back at Dave. "My sorry-ass ca—" A connection seemed to register in the cop's mind. "It's over, man. It's over. And it's all your fault." He pointed the barrel at Dave.

"No!" Heather screamed, running at Landers.

A shot rang out as she placed her kick. Landers shouted and fell, his weapon skimming across the floor.

Heather turned to see Powers, holstering his gun. "Would you mind calling an ambulance for this piece of trash?" he asked Diana. "He'll be living behind bars for a long time, and his wife can come out of hiding—wherever she is." He bent down and cuffed Landers.

Suddenly, Dave stood in front of her, with his arms out, and she could think of no one else. "Heather?" She ran to him. Then he was holding her, rocking her. Kissing her everywhere, treating her bruised cheek gently.

She glanced at Hank lying on the floor groaning. "I guess every family has a black sheep."

LATER THAT EVENING, after all the statements, all the legal matters and after speaking with Mary Beth and the children for an hour, Heather drove herself home. Dave had kissed her and then continued his shift. And she realized that this is how a regular patrol officer lived—day after day, shift after shift—alternating between readiness and a high adrenaline rush. Never knowing what would really happen on any particular day, but always anticipating the worst. Not an easy way of life. Lots of stress.

George had not exemplified a good cop. Her dad had been a show-off who liked to throw his weight around.

Dave's attitude and actions defined good cop. And if he'd allow it, she'd help him keep his balance for the rest of his life. She'd help him shrug off his uniform when his day ended. Keep him sane and happy.

She pulled into her driveway and sat there with the engine running. *She'd never told him.* And yet...he kept hanging around. "You're the biggest coward under the sun," she murmured.

She checked the time. His shift was almost over, and she pressed her autodial to his cell.

Still in uniform, he showed up forty-five minutes later. Heather waited in the driveway leaning against her car, studying him as he got out of his.

Fatigue had settled on his face...until he spotted her and his smile washed away the effects of the busy shift.

She opened her arms, and he was there. "I love you, Dave. I've loved you for a long time."

"I know. At least, I'd hoped. But please say it again."

There were no more barriers. She trusted him. Dave was everything she wanted. He was the right man for her.

"Marry me, Heather." Like a heartfelt prayer spoken aloud. "I feel like I've been waiting forever."

"Of course, I will." She kissed him, then sighed as she leaned against him. "Let's get married and have a quiet, peaceful life."

Dave laughed out loud. "A peaceful life with Heather Marshall? I know it will be a full life. And a fulfilling life. But quiet? Somehow, sweetheart, I don't think so."

She looked into his face and thought about all the excitement ahead of them.

Her laughter joined Dave's. "Hmm…maybe you're right. But at least we won't be bored."

He kissed her. "Say it again."

She knew exactly what he meant. "I love you, Dave. And I'll be telling you so for the rest of our lives."

"Promise?" he asked.

"Yes."

"And I promise to do the same."

A promise she could count on. She didn't need anything more.

Experience the anticipation, the thrill of the chase and the sheer rush of falling in love! Turn the page for a sneak preview of a new book from Harlequin Romance, THE REBEL PRINCE by Raye Morgan. On sale August 29 wherever books are sold.

"OH, NO!"

The reaction slipped out before Emma Valentine could stop it, for there stood the very man she most wanted to avoid seeing again.

He didn't look any happier to see her.

"Well, come on, get on board," he said gruffly. "I won't bite." One eyebrow rose. "Though I might nibble a little," he added, mostly to amuse himself.

But she wasn't paying any attention to what he was saying. She was staring at him, taking in the royal blue uniform he was wearing, with gold braid and glistening badges decorating the sleeves, epaulettes and an upright collar. Ribbons and medals covered the breast of the short, fitted jacket. A gold-encrusted sabre hung at his side. And suddenly it was clear to her who this man really was.

She gulped wordlessly. Reaching out, he took her elbow and pulled her aboard. The doors slid closed. And finally she found her tongue.

"You…you're the prince."

He nodded, barely glancing at her. "Yes. Of course."

She raised a hand and covered her mouth for a moment. "I should have known."

"Of course you should have. I don't know why you didn't." He punched the ground-floor button to get the elevator moving again, then turned to look down at her. "A relatively bright five-year-old child would have tumbled to the truth right away."

Her shock faded as her indignation at his tone asserted itself. He might be the prince, but he was still just as annoying as he had been earlier that day.

"A relatively bright five-year-old child without a bump on the head from a badly thrown water polo ball, maybe," she said defensively. She wasn't feeling woozy any longer and she wasn't about to let him bully her, no matter how royal he was. "I was unconscious half the time."

"And just clueless the other half, I guess," he said, looking bemused.

The arrogance of the man was really galling.

"I suppose you think your 'royalness' is so obvious it sort of shimmers around you for all to see?" she challenged. "Or better yet, oozes from your pores like…like sweat on a hot day?"

"Something like that," he acknowledged calmly. "Most people tumble to it pretty quickly. In fact, it's hard to hide even when I want to avoid dealing with it."

"Poor baby," she said, still resenting his manner. "I guess that works better with injured people who are half asleep." Looking at him, she felt a strange emotion she couldn't identify. It was as though she wanted to prove something to him, but she wasn't sure what. "And anyway, you know you did your best to fool me," she added.

His brows knit together as though he really didn't know what she was talking about. "I didn't do a thing."

"You told me your name was Monty."

"It is." He shrugged. "I have a lot of names. Some of them are too rude to be spoken to my face, I'm sure." He glanced at her sideways, his hand on the hilt of his sabre. "Perhaps you're contemplating one of those right now."

You bet I am.

That was what she would like to say. But it suddenly occurred to her that she was supposed to be working for this man. If she wanted to keep the job of coronation chef, maybe she'd better keep her opinions to herself. So she clamped her mouth shut, took a deep breath and looked away, trying hard to calm down.

The elevator ground to a halt and the doors slid open laboriously. She moved to step forward, hoping to make her escape, but his hand shot out again and caught her elbow.

"Wait a minute. *You're* a woman," he said, as though that thought had just presented itself to him.

"That's a rare ability for insight you have there, Your Highness," she snapped before she could stop herself. And then she winced. She was going to have to do better than that if she was going to keep this relationship on an even keel.

But he was ignoring her dig. Nodding, he stared at her with a speculative gleam in his golden eyes. "I've been looking for a woman, but you'll do."

She blanched, stiffening. "I'll do for what?"

He made a head gesture in a direction she knew was opposite of where she was going and his grip tightened on her elbow.

"Come with me," he said abruptly, making it an order.

She dug in her heels, thinking fast. She didn't much like orders. "Wait! I can't. I have to get to the kitchen."

"Not yet. I need you."

"You what?" Her breathless gasp of surprise was soft, but she knew he'd heard it.

"I need you," he said firmly. "Oh, don't look so shocked. I'm not planning to throw you into the hay and have my way with you. I need you for something a bit more mundane than that."

She felt color rushing into her cheeks and she silently begged it to stop. Here she was, formless and stodgy in her chef's whites. No makeup, no stiletto heels. Hardly the picture of the femmes fatales he was undoubtedly used to. The likelihood that he would have any carnal interest in her was remote at best. To have him think she was hysterically defending her virtue was humiliating.

"Well, what if I don't want to go with you?" she said in hopes of deflecting his attention from her blush.

"Too bad."

"What?"

Amusement sparkled in his eyes. He was certainly enjoying this. And that only made her more determined to resist him.

"I'm the prince, remember? And we're in the castle. My orders take precedence. It's that old pesky divine rights thing."

Her jaw jutted out. Despite her embarrassment, she couldn't let that pass.

"Over my free will? Never!"

Exasperation filled his face.

"Hey, call out the historians. Someone will write a book about you and your courageous principles." His eyes glittered sardonically. "But in the meantime, Emma Valentine, you're coming with me."

COMING NEXT MONTH

#1368 ANGELS OF THE BIG SKY • Roz Denny Fox
The Cloud Chasers
Widow Marlee Stein returns to Montana with her young daughter, ready to help out with Cloud Chasers, the flying service owned by her twin brother, Mick Callen. Because of Mick's surgery, Marlee takes over piloting duties, including mercy flights—and immediately finds herself in conflict with one of his clients, ranger Wylie Ames. Too bad Marlee's so attracted to a man she doesn't even want to *like!*

#1369 MAN FROM MONTANA • Brenda Mott
Single Father
Kara never would've dreamed she'd be a widow so young—or that she could find room in her heart for anyone besides her husband. And then Derrick moved in across the street....

#1370 THE RETURN OF DAVID McKAY • Ann Evans
Heart of the Rockies
David McKay thought he'd seen the last of Broken Yoke when he left for Hollywood—until a pilgrimage into the mountains to scatter his grandfather's ashes forced him to return and face his first love, Adriana D'Angelo. That's when he realized the price he'd paid for his ambition. And how much a second chance at happiness would change his life...

#1371 SMALL-TOWN SECRETS • Margaret Watson
Hometown U.S.A.
It took Gabe Townsend seven years to return to Sturgeon Falls after the fateful car accident. He would never have come back if he hadn't had to. Because he still loved Kendall, and she was his best friend's wife.

#1372 MAKE-BELIEVE COWBOY • Terry McLaughlin
Bright Lights, Big Sky
A widow with a kid and a mountain of debt. A good-looking man everyone *thought* they knew. Meeting for the first time under the wide-open skies of Montana!

#1373 MR. IMPERFECT • Karina Bliss
Going Back
The last will and testament of Kezia's beloved grandmother is the only thing that could drag bad boy Christian Kelly back to the hometown that had brought him only misery....

HSRCNM0806